20 SHORT STORIES

CLIVE ZIETMAN

"What we anticipate seldom occurs. What we least expected generally happens."

Benjamin Disraeli.

CONTENTS

THE OLD MAN

Nobody took too much notice of the old man who frequented the park every day. He looked odd but regular visitors to the park had become used to him and treated him very much as part of the furniture. The man's scrawny body was always draped in a filthy grey raincoat, whatever the weather. He wore a battered trilby with somewhat incongruous new Nike trainers. He limped. His deeply-lined face had the sort of hunted look that one might typically associate with dipsomaniac paranoia but the old man was not paranoid. Nor did he drink alcohol. Anyone who took a few seconds to glance at the man assumed that he was a tramp.

Occasionally teenagers would laugh at the man and throw things at him but, for the most part, he was ignored by passers-by, old and young alike. He would most commonly sit on a bench near the duck pond, reading a book and minding his own business. When the weather was inclement the man retreated to a sheltered area; his favorite spot was the disused cricket pavilion on the far side of the park. On some days he could be seen sitting on a swing or perhaps on the rotating witch's hat in the children's play area. The equipment there had fallen into disrepair and was in desperate need of renovation and lubrication. It squeaked so much that no one could bear to use it. Except for the old man who sat on the witch's hat, reading his book. Now and again he peered from one side or the other and then resumed reading.

One Tuesday morning, after receiving a complaint from a concerned mother, the recently-appointed park-keeper approached the man and asked him to move away from the children's play area. The man complied. He did so in a mild-mannered fashion and not, as the park-keeper expected of a vagrant, in a way that might involve a violent outburst. After their short exchange of words it began to rain. The park keeper disappeared off to his hut to brew a pot of tea and the man wandered towards his customary haunt – a bench situated under cover, just outside the pavilion. A few hours later, as the man lay in a slumped back position on the bench, he was approached by the concerned mother. She had assumed that the man had vacated the park, so her blood pressure rose upon spotting him. It soon became obvious that she was spoiling for a fight.

"Why are you still 'ere?" she shouted. "I was told that you were goin' to be moved on. Why are you 'ere?"

"I'm terribly sorry," replied the man in a voice that was so well spoken the woman was taken aback. His tone was disarmingly reasonable. "I've just been reading my book. I love coming to the park. I had no reason to believe that I was causing offence to anyone. I certainly haven't been making a nuisance of myself."

"Listen," said the woman, "you can't charm me into thinkin' that you're not up to mischief. I know your type. Why would a grown man like you hang around the park?   D'you like watching the little girls playing on the swings? Or are little boys your thing?"

"I do like children," said the man, "but not in the way you imply."   He gently scratched his beard whilst composing his next sentence. "What's troubling you so much? You sound so aggrieved. You don't need to be"

"Just listen to me you pervert," replied the woman. "I want you to leave the park and never come back. Do I make myself clear? If you don't clear off I'll call the police"

The old man said nothing by way of response but stood up and carefully placed his book into a neat brown leather satchel. He stared blankly at the woman and wandered off towards the park exit that led onto a quiet suburban road.

Dusk was approaching and the sky became filled with dark grey and purple clouds. The old man headed towards a small parade of shops. Three were shut but the fourth, a fish and chip shop, was just opening. It was empty. Just before entering, the man caught sight of his reflection in the shop window. He paused for a moment, mildly fascinated by his own shocking appearance – his dishevelled ginger and grey beard, his craggy pock-marked face and his cloudy bluish eyes. He was no portrait. But how had it come to this? Why would no one listen? He had once been so confident that they would.

The fish and chip shop owner was a tubby cheerful soul with bright red cheeks and a heart-warming smile. "The usual?" he asked.

"Please," replied the old man, handing over a fistful of rather dirty coins. The chip shop owner shovelled an extra large portion of fat chips into a bag together with a pickled egg and handed the bag to the old man. "Thank you very much indeed," said the man politely. "This is just what I needed."

The man then shuffled off down the road into the maze of near-by suburban streets, munching his chips. His limp, which had grown progressively worse in recent weeks, was more pronounced. When he had finished the chips the man carefully folded up the paper wrapping and put it in his pocket.

He wandered on for more than an hour, gradually leaving the suburbs and making his way into one of the far less salubrious parts of the city. Here the sodium street lighting seemed murkier and the buildings were scruffier and dingier. The neat, semi-detached houses gave way to poorly-maintained terraced homes and dark alleyways. As the man approached one alleyway he found himself accosted by an aging whore. The woman's make-up was dreadful; her face was heavily powdered, giving her a pale and cadaverous look, which was offset by shocking cherry red lips that protruded slightly like puckered wedges of rubber.

"Looking for a good time?" she whispered in a husky voice that purported to be alluring.

The man smiled politely and gently brushed past the whore, continuing on his way. He headed towards the docks where the streets became even darker and more deserted. It started to rain again and gusts of sea breeze sent swirls of leaves and litter across the streets. The man gathered his coat with both hands to shield his thin body from the elements as he carried on. He eventually found himself outside a giant, derelict warehouse and entered via a large space where a window had once been – the glass having long since been smashed to pieces. The ruined brick building appeared to have had its guts ripped out; the ground floor was littered with broken, rusty machinery, empty crates, mounds of rotting corrugated paper and cardboard and other general rubbish. On the far side of the warehouse there was a cast-iron spiral staircase.

The man headed in that direction and ascended at a slow pace, hampered by his limp and the damp slippery steps. Ten minutes later he made it to the roof of the warehouse. The rain pounded down and the wind tugged at the man's clothing. He walked towards a parapet that surrounding the top of the warehouse and stared down into the abyss below. He stood for a while, as his rugged face became a patchwork of streaming tears and raindrops that dripped into his sodden dirty beard. After taking a few deep breaths of salty air he retreated from the edge and, after letting out a short sigh, returned to the stairway and made his way downwards. Not now. Not tonight. There was still time.

The old man headed back to the park where he would find some shelter for the night. In the weeks and months that would follow more obscene abuse would be hurled at him and more children would throw things at him and laugh. Which was a pity. Because the man was the Messiah. But nobody believed him.

The Turning Point

The atmosphere in the room was warm. The combination of subdued lighting and comfortable chairs was an advantage. The discussion had followed a somewhat familiar pattern, and so far there had been no surprises.

"I decided to call it Operation Barbarossa."

"Why? What was Barbarossa?" asked Dr Schwartz in a voice that displayed genuine interest, despite his flagging energy level. He needed another strong coffee, but it would have to wait. Unless he engaged and showed a degree of enthusiasm, this would not go well.

"You mean you have never heard of Frederick Barbarossa? You were not taught in school about Frederick the First? He was a Holy Roman Emperor who lived in the 12th century. He was without a doubt one of the greatest and most charismatic leaders of his era – Germany's equivalent of Richard the Lionheart. He possessed remarkable strength of character and an awe-inspiring personality, but above all he had vision. He saw that Germany would never thrive so long as it remained little more than an unruly collection of self-governing states. There was too much in-fighting. In order to develop and flourish, Germany needed to exist at a higher level; it had to be unified in order to be anything at all. No one in history gave Germany a greater sense of purpose and unity than me, but Frederick the First was certainly my inspiration."

"And so you named your most ambitious enterprise after him."

"Yes. I code-named our glorious venture into Russia Operation Barbarossa because I could think of no better title for what was and remains the largest and most successful military operation in human history."

"And what did Operation Barbarossa involve? Do remind me. I should, of course, be better acquainted with the facts."

"On 22nd June 1941, I ordered nearly four million troops to commence the invasion of Russia. We had been planning the invasion for more than a year. Meticulous work went into every aspect of the operation. The movement of our troops took place over a front that stretched a distance of nearly three-thousand kilometres. We deployed astonishing resources – six hundred thousand motorised vehicles including tanks, armoured cars and troop carriers and nearly seven hundred and fifty thousand horses. It was a magnificent display of force. The world witnessed the true might of the Fatherland, and thereafter no one could ever doubt our supreme power, our superiority or our desire to create a new world – a world purer and far better than the one that so badly needed replacing. Even though I say it myself, Operation Barbarossa was a work of genius."

"But, presumably, Operation Barbarossa carried a short-term objective as well as forming part of a much greater scheme?"

"Oh, yes. My short term plan was very clear and focused. I regarded it as absolutely essential for there to be a root and branch de-modernisation of the entire Soviet Union. My aim was to convert it into a de-populated, de-industrialised agrarian colony, a dominion that could serve all the expanding needs of the Fatherland in terms of food, slave labour and of course other natural resources. The Soviets commanded a vast range of minerals and oil reserves that would unquestionably be of huge strategic importance to the struggle that lay ahead. I had complete faith in the Wehrmacht and the Luftwaffe to bring the Soviet Untermenschen to their knees within months, even weeks. After our glorious victories in Western Europe, that is what I fully expected to happen. And that is precisely what did happen."

Dr Schwartz paused at this point and plucked his steel-rimmed reading glasses from the top pocket of his shirt. He then rummaged around in his right trouser pocket and produced a small piece of chamois leather. Deep in thought he then started to clean his lenses with the cloth, rubbing them gently at first and then more vigorously. Saying nothing, he donned the spectacles, positioning them low on his nose so he could look over them. He then started penning notes on a pad that was attached to a clipboard. He scribbled quickly, occasionally staring upwards as if seeking divine inspiration. It had been a long day and he wanted to bring this to a conclusion. He was acutely aware that it was nearly a quarter past six and that he had theatre tickets for a play that began at seven forty-five. He had promised his wife he would not let her down the way he had far too often in the past.

"So, that was the plan. The Great Plan. But things did not go as you expected them to, did they? The German forces made great headway in 1941, but you underestimated the resourcefulness of the Soviets and misjudged the ferocity of the harsh Russian winter, didn't you? Operation Barbarossa was a disaster, wasn't it?"

"Could I have a glass of water, please?"

"Yes, of course. Certainly," said Dr Schwartz. He reached over to a small jug of tap water and filled a plastic cup that he then carefully handed over. The cup was received with a slightly trembling hand, and as Dr Schwartz lent closer he could see tiny droplets of nervous perspiration on the craggy face of his interviewee. He had not intended to make him feel ill at ease, but his questions were regrettably having that effect.

"No, that is not correct."

"Not correct? The invasion of Russia was not a disaster? Are you serious? Is that what you're suggesting?"

"No. You misunderstand me."

"I know. You say that you would have been victorious if not for the weakness of others. You say, don't you, that the plan was good, but that you were let down by your inept generals – Von Rundstedt, Von Bock and Von Leeb, for example?

You presumably say that Operation Barbarossa was sound, but ended in defeat because of the failings of those to whom you entrusted the task of winning at all costs."

"No. My generals did their duty and without them we would not have secured victory."

"Victory?" exclaimed Dr Schwartz, raising his voice. "What victory? You call the loss of millions of German servicemen a victory? Most respectable historians take the view that the invasion of Russia proved to be nothing less than a colossal mistake – a grotesque miscalculation that, with the benefit of hindsight, was undoubtedly a hugely significant turning point in the course of the war. Is that not the correct analysis?"

"Of course not. After the fall of Moscow, it was plain sailing. The defeat of the Soviet Union was complete."

Dr Schwartz held up his hand to signal that he wanted to hear no more until he finished his note. There was no question that this was an extraordinary departure from what he and his colleagues had expected. He reached for the jug of water again and this time poured himself a drink. He needed a moment or two in order to think about how best to frame his next line of questions. This was not in the script. He decided to proceed in a tone that was firm, without being too aggressive. He sipped his water and continued.

"The fall of Moscow, you say?" He raised his left eyebrow by a fraction as he spoke.

"Yes."

Dr Schwartz winced slightly and paused.

"But there was no fall of Moscow, was there?" The temperature in the room seemed to plummet in an instant. The question produced no immediate answer. "The siege of Stalingrad failed and the tide of the campaign turned at that point. What do you mean when you refer to the fall of Moscow?" Dr Schwartz stared hard at his patient. Over the last few weeks, the delusions had become much more elaborate and detailed, yet were still consistently anchored in historically accurate facts. When Mr. Lenz was first admitted to the institution in June, boldly asserting that he was Napoleon, he had described to Dr Schwartz, with rich and colourful examples, his battle experiences, his love life and even minute details of his everyday life. Everything he related had been coherent and consistent with historical records. The same was true when he suddenly became Hitler, except Mr. Lenz's fantasy world was turning into a delusion within a delusion. "There was no fall of Moscow, and you are not Adolf Hitler, are you, Mr. Lenz?"

Mr. Lenz appeared to be lost for words, his confidence suddenly shattered. He looked crestfallen as his head dropped down into his chest. He was silent for a minute or so. Dr Schwartz said nothing but simply continued to hold his stare, waiting for his patient to respond. Gradually, as if being lifted in stages by a clumsy ratchet, Mr. Lenz's head moved upwards inch by inch. Once in an upright position, he stared back at Dr Schwartz. His eyes were bloodshot and webbed with veins. They drilled into the eyes of Dr

Schwartz as if he were suddenly possessed. His hair flopped across his sweaty forehead and he spoke brightly, with a remarkably polished American accent:

"I just want to do God's will. And He's allowed me to go up to the mountain. And I've looked over. And I've seen the Promised Land. I may not get there with you. But I want you to know tonight, that we, as a people, will get to the Promised Land."

Dr Schwartz smiled sweetly. He replaced his glasses in his shirt pocket and put down his clip board. If he hurried, he would still make it to the theatre in time.

AN AUSPICIOUS DAY

The two fat bluebottles that buzzed noisily around the room were starting to irritate Lee immensely. He was trying his level best to think as clearly as he could. He was attempting to concentrate on what he had to do, yet all he could seem to focus on was how he could swat those two goddam filthy flies. One hit the window at high velocity but, with the robustness that seemed to armour plate the chitin exoskeletons of all such creatures, the insect bounced off the glass unscathed and continued with its Brownian motion through the warm November air. It was stuffy in the room, but he didn't want to open the widow – not quite yet, even though there were compelling reasons to do so; it would be good to let some fresh air into the room and let the flies out, but he would leave it a few minutes. There was certainly no rush.

He took another swig from the bottle of coke that he had brought up to the sixth floor with him. An empty that he had discarded twenty minutes earlier lay on the grubby floor and it had started to attract the attention of the second bluebottle. He needed that second drink already, as his mouth was parched. Was it the just heat, or was he feeling a little bit edgy? Perhaps it was a combination of the two. Globules of sweat had begun to appear on his forehead, neck and the palms of his hands. He gulped the liquid greedily and even though the drink was no longer ice cold, he welcomed it.

There was something comforting about being shut in an enclosed space surrounded by boxes and boxes of books. In some irrational way, these buff-coloured cuboids stacked together like breeze blocks felt like a protective shield. He guessed that they actually might, in theory at least, provide a form of cover if someone were to interrupt him unexpectedly. It was like being in a secret library, a reading room in which all the books were inaccessible and out of bounds. Literature, literature everywhere, but not a page to read. He toyed with the idea of ripping open one of the cardboard boxes at random, just to fish out a textbook or two in order to distract himself for a few minutes. Even though he had always hated writing, especially essays at school, he thought about the sort of books he loved: war books, thrillers and political stuff, too. He quickly dismissed the notion. He had a newspaper, and although he had thumbed through it twice already, he began to do so for a third time. As he flicked through the pages, his eyes focused on a large advertisement for the new convertible Thunderbird. He had missed the ad when skimming through the pages earlier that day. If he ever managed to settle down for good and make some money he'd buy one of those. It was good to dream. There was something special about convertible cars. He had never driven one, but he enjoyed the idea of being in one. He could imagine the wind rushing through his hair and the sense of openness and liberation it would bring.

He took slow, deep breaths in order to maintain his sense of calm. A tingle of excitement was starting to well up inside his stomach, but that was okay. That was normal. His brother John had told him about the technique of controlling your breathing as part of a yoga-type procedure through which you could concentrate properly on the activity of your mind and body. Those who really mastered the art could even lower their heart rate, quite dramatically in some cases. John had explained this to him in some detail, along with all the other things that he learnt as a marine and wanted to pass along to his brother. A flashback suddenly came to him of the two boys messing around one weekend not long after John had enlisted. It was August and very hot. John had come back for a couple of days of leave and had let him try on his helmet, which felt empowering. They had had such fun together, taking photos of each other in uniform and fooling around the way they had when they were little kids. What a shame that John could not be with him now. He would have been so proud of him. Lee loved and admired his brother, even though John was a goody-two-shoes by comparison. John never got into trouble. Lee, on the other hand, had had a bellyful of trouble. He was trouble.

Inspired perhaps by the bright daylight outside, he then had an even older flashback of going for a skinny dip with John and two of John's girlfriends during one glorious summer. It was fun and exciting. He cast his mind back to how they had messed around in a secluded lake not far from his place. The water had that curious effect on him that only nature can produce – it was both warm and refreshing. He could do with a splash of invigorating water right now, he thought. Those scenes of merriment seemed like ancient history. Many of the details were surprisingly vivid, while others had grown hazy with the passage of time. They had become like a flickering cine film in his mind's eye. The movie was not black and white, however. It was rose-coloured.

As if to grab his attention, one of the bluebottles suddenly whacked into his right arm and then took refuge on a dusty spot just underneath the windowsill. Lee inched his hand towards his newspaper whilst keeping a close eye on the unsuspecting fly. Without making a sound he rolled the newspaper into a hard, truncheon shape and carefully curled his fingers around the base. With a vice-like grip he clutched the makeshift weapon and, in the blink of an eye, arced his arm across his body with a devastating smack, killing the mite before it had half a chance to escape. Its flattened corpse dropped onto the floorboards. The other fly zipped off to the far side of the room as though it knew its demise would be imminent if it hung around too long.

Just as he picked up his bottle of coke again, he heard a faint muffle of voices coming in the direction of the room. They were far too distinct to have originated from anywhere but the corridor immediately outside. As the sound grew nearer, he felt a definite sense of danger. He heard footsteps, too, and decided to scuttle rapidly into a dark corner of the room in the style of a cockroach. Within a second he had adopted a crouching position behind a pyramid of large boxes in a secluded part of the room. He held his breath and waited. Had his luck run out? He could hear the voices of two men – local, middle-aged, uneducated.

"D'you hear that Frank? I'm sure I heard a thud o' some sort. A noise like someone hit somethin'."

"I didn't hear nothin'. You must be imaginin' things a'gen. You're goin' soft in the head."

"No, Frank, I heard somethin'. I'm damn sure I did."

"Could have been a mouse or critters. There was an infestation in the basement few months back."

"Guess you're probably right. Anyways, as I was saying to Clarence, I says, 'Clarence, you ain't got any right to say them kinda things. You don't know shit about this here work schedule.'"

The voices and footsteps tapered off into the distance and Lee breathed a sigh of relief. He should have restrained himself when bashing that bluebottle, but he knew his weaknesses, and lack of self-control was one of them.

He stood up and stretched his arms upwards, then sideways. For no particular reason, he also decided to do a few press-ups. After limbering up, he stood once more and yawned. The caffeine from the coke was keeping him alert but he had not slept well the night before, and he was not in the peak form he had hoped for. He was irritated that his palms still felt sweaty. He looked at his watch for the third time in as many minutes. It was 12:27. He moved towards the window, opened it and was struck not just by the wafts of fresh air that swept into the room but by the sheer size and noise of the crowds below. Two police motorcyclists came into view ahead of the motorcade that was sure to emerge from round the corner at any moment. He wiped his palms on the sleeves of his shirt and reached for his rifle. The second bluebottle swooped past his head, through the open window and out into the sunshine.

THE ROAD TO HELL

"How long will it take us to git to Disneyland, Pa?" asked Ryan. His father was loading a case of Coca Cola into the monster-sized trunk of his five-litre all-wheel drive with several plastic carrier bags filled with treats and snacks for the journey. Distracted by his activity and the barking of the German Shepherd next door, Hank failed to hear what his son was asking.

"I said, Pa, how long is the car journey to Disneyland?" He wiped his nose on his sleeve as he spoke.

"Bout eight 'ours by my reckonin'," answered his father in a voice that was discernibly breathless as a result of his exertions. "Doubt if we'll git there until well after nightfall. Now you jus' git in the back of the car and don't start a'fightin' with your sister. Las' time we went away on vacation you was unbearable, the both of you. I ain't havin' that agin do you hear?"

"Sure thing, Pa," replied Ryan with his head bowed. Ryan clambered up into the vehicle and sat down on the spacious back seat next to Megan who was far too preoccupied by a huge bag of sickly-looking pink candies to notice the arrival of her older brother. A minute or so later their father opened the driver's door, his bright red baseball cap narrowly missing the top of the door frame as he squeezed his two hundred and fifty pound bulk into position.   They were soon joined by their mother, Cindy, a creature whose elephantine proportions were more than a match for her spouse.   She sat down with a grunt and what sounded like a flatulent emission of methane.

"Hey hun, let's git this show on the road," she said cheerfully, slapping the palm of her left hand on her husband's chubby right thigh.   Hank responded immediately by turning the ignition key, pressing hard on the gas pedal and thundering out of the driveway of their home towards the main road that led westward out of the suburbs. It was baking hot outside, hotter than any summer in living memory. The blistering heat took its toll with unusual side-effects; the tarmac on the road was sweating spherules of black pus and the tires of Hank's vehicle seemed to burn rubber at every turn. He turned the air conditioning onto full blast, set the satellite navigation system and switched on the sound system that burst into life with a gloomy number by Chris Rea. Ten minutes later they were well on their way. Hank switched his mental state to autopilot, positioning his left elbow on the ledge of his open window. His sixth Marlboro of the day was wedged firmly between his nicotine-stained fingertips.

"I love the smell of smouldering tobacco first thing in the morning!" he laughed.

An hour or so into the journey, with the car on cruise control and Hank's mind away with the fairies rather than focused on the road ahead, the speeding vehicle skidded sharply to the left without warning. Fearing that one of his tires had blown, Hank pulled the vehicle to the side of the road and climbed down to look for the cause of the problem and for damage. He marched around the car and noticed blood and brown gunge on the nearside front tire. He looked back down the road where he could quickly make out the remains of a decapitated skunk, squashed flat in the middle of the road. He checked for possible dents caused to the bodywork of the car by the unfortunate creature, but found none and returned to his seat.

"What's up, hun?" asked Cindy who managed to simultaneously speak and demolish a large banana with the bovine sideways motion of her jaw.

"Nothin', hun. Jus' killed a lousy skunk that must'a decided the road was a good place to loiter. There ain't much a'him left now," he added. "Not sure why, but seeing that raw meat has made me kinda peckish. Who says we grab a few buckets o' chicken an' fries at the next KFC we come to?"

Hank's suggestion was met with a chorus of approval and an hour later the family found themselves tucking into copious quantities of fatty comestibles. Ryan and Megan wiped their greasy hands on the car seat. The unwanted packaging, used napkins and chewed bones were randomly jettisoned out of the car windows.

As the sun started to descend in the west, Hank ploughed onwards into the gathering gloom on a long straight highway that seemed to lead nowhere. According to the satellite navigation, they were driving through a long strip of desert. The road seemed to be entirely devoid of human activity. Hank's wife was slumped at an awkward angle, snoring like a rattlesnake and dribbling down her chin whilst the children amused themselves a computer game called Death Zombies. Hank drove like an automaton, humming to himself and occasionally nudging his spouse with his right arm to adjust the position of her corpulent torso and to stop her from snoring. Further along the road, when the sun was little more than an occluded bloodshot disc, and the surrounding countryside was enveloped in darkness, a warning light appeared on Hank's dashboard to indicate that he was low on fuel. Having passed several gas stations without stopping, he cursed to himself under his breath, knowing he had no choice but to carry on. He had a spare canister of gas in the trunk, but it was a last-gasp gallon that he did not want to rely on. After another thirty miles, however, his thirsty gas-guzzler ground to a halt and Hank had to get out and make use of his emergency fuel.

"Watsa problem hun?" asked his wife, waking up from her slumber as he climbed back into the car and slammed the door with a thud. "I need to git us to a gas station," he replied. "I'm sure we'll see one soon." Hank restarted the engine and continued driving. A few minutes later the headlamps shed light on the mouth of a large tunnel. He was confused. "This here tunnel is kinda odd. It ain't showing up on the sat nav, and it seems a weird spot for a tunnel anyhow." Cindy said nothing. He thought to himself that this was the last place on earth he wanted to grind to a halt for lack of gas, but there was nothing to do but drive on and hope for the best.

Hank set the car's cruise control at a fuel-efficient fifty-five miles per hour and prayed that all would be fine. A few minutes later the gas light came on again, just as the tunnel started to slope gently downward. The tunnel started to bend a little, as though on a wide spiral trajectory. Hank tried to override the cruise control by gently pressing on the brake pedal, discovering, to his horror, that it would not respond. Panicked, he tried other controls in the car such as the handbrake, but they, too, were unresponsive. He calmed himself as best he could, then spoke with an unmistakable tremor in his voice.

"Cindy, this car is out of control. I can't stop the freaking thing. The brakes ain't working, it's driving itself along at fifty-five, but I can't stop this piece of shit. Hell, I can't even slow it down." Just as he finished his sentence, the car's central locking system clicked into place as if the vehicle possessed a mind of its own. Hank could feel that he was losing control; his stomach was tightly gripped by piercing cramps and his bowels were turning to water. At that second the car's dashboard lit up with every single warning indicator, a display of multi-coloured lights. Hank looked on in disbelief.

"What the fuck is going on?" screamed Cindy, infected by her husband's panic.

"I don't know," he replied solemnly. "It's like some kinda nightmare. I don't understand."

The car careered further into the tunnel, the gradient of which became noticeably steeper and the curves more pronounced. Hank glanced down at the speedometer and saw that the needle had crept up to sixty-five. Hank began sweating profusely, clutching the steering wheel with tight fists and all of his strength, as if he were clinging onto life itself. His eyes caught a glimpse of his children in the rear view mirror – Ryan and Megan's terrified faces were drained of blood, white with a spattering of colour from the lights of the dashboard. Their eyes bulged in their sockets. Equally panicked, Cindy frantically attempted to open the door on her side but discovered that the handle was useless. The door was jammed.

"We can't get out. We're trapped. We're gonna die," she announced with resignation. "I jus' don't understand. What have we done wrong?"

Hank said nothing in return, but simply stared ahead into the black throat of the tunnel that seemed to devour them. The car was now going at seventy miles per hour, and the downward slope of the road had become frighteningly steep. The bends were even sharper and Hank expected to crash at any moment. Instead the car accelerated deeper and deeper into the Earth. His final glimpse, from the corner of his eye, was of Cindy's rigid, petrified body.

"We gonna die?" whimpered Ryan a minute later, his safety belt digging into the girth of his waist. But his feeble question fell deaf on the ears of his parents, whose heads were now slumped forward onto their chests, lifeless and oblivious to the high-speed helter-skelter ride. Megan, too, had passed out, and only Ryan bore witness to the glow from the orange inferno below as the car plummeted downwards at an almost vertical angle.

DIEU ET MON DROIT

The colour of Mr. Henry Rutherford QC's wig contrasted starkly with that of his learned junior seated behind him. His was a rather odd mixture of grey and dirty yellow, whereas that of his young assistant was silvery white. The difference in hues stemmed not just from the vast gulf in age between the two headpieces, but also from the fact that Mr. Rutherford was extremely partial to cigarettes - the unfiltered Turkish variety that stank to high heaven and stained everything that came into contact with the malodorous smoke they produced. His wig of aged distinction, his ruddy cheeks and his double chin gave Mr. Rutherford an air of gravitas that bordered on that of a caricature - an image that he did nothing to minimise. He well knew that the juries he addressed inevitably identified with, and secretly respected, the fictional advocates that formed the bedrock of television court dramas. A hint of Rumpole did Mr. Rutherford no harm at all.

As Mr. Rutherford stood up to speak, following a tortuously protracted interjection by his opponent, he was acutely aware that he was cross-examining at the worst possible time of day, for it was mid-afternoon on a Friday. After the lunchtime recess the minds of the jurors would inevitably begin to wander. Half of them would be planning the weekend ahead, which in many ways was understandable given the turgid and stuffy atmosphere of the court room setting they had endured for the past week. It was essential that he produced some drama, something to wake them from their reveries. Added to that, the judge also seemed to be losing concentration, so it was therefore essential that he brought matters to a head.

"And so, Reverend Short, it's right, is it not, that at or about ten past ten on the evening of 1st November last year, you drove to the Esso petrol station in Sandy Lane, Newton in your grey Volvo estate motorcar?" asked Mr. Rutherford, peering in a pronounced fashion over his reading glasses as he spoke. He smiled at the defendant as he completed the sentence, as if to charm him.

"That is correct," answered the Reverend without a hint of emotion.

"And, upon your arrival at the said petrol station, you filled up not just the tank of your motorcar, but a blue plastic container, a vessel that held approximately one gallon of fuel. That's also correct, is it not?"

"That's also correct, except that the container was green," responded Reverend Short, once again in a monotone voice that revealed nothing.

"Yes, green. Of course. Thank you for that," said Mr. Rutherford, pleased that the Reverend had picked up on the deliberate error, thus demonstrating that he was paying attention. "And then, after paying for the petrol you returned to your vehicle and drove directly to the house of Miss Joyce Flowers at 34 Ridgeway Crescent, Newton, where you arrived at approximately ten thirty. That's right, isn't it?"

"That's not quite right, Mr. Rutherford. I stopped along the way."

"You stopped along the way? Please do enlighten us as to where you stopped."

"I realised that I had forgotten to buy matches at the petrol station. I stopped at a late-night supermarket on the way to Ridgeway Crescent. I bought some matches and, as far as I recall, a packet of extra-strong mints."

"I see. Before we go on to what happened next, Reverend, please tell us, if you would, how you would describe Miss Flowers, or should I say the late Miss Flowers? What did she look like? What kind of person was she?"

"Well, she was a spinster in her sixties. Not someone who you'd describe as being in the best of health. She was of medium build with long, jet black hair - dyed of course. She kept cats, lots of them. She was unhygienic and rude, and she was what you might call a practitioner of the dark arts."

Mr. Rutherford paused quite deliberately at this point to let the jury absorb Reverend Short's choice of words. He pursed his podgy lips, an affectation he often deployed when he was about to ask a particularly probing question, and then faced the jury, even though he was still quizzing the defendant.

"The dark arts, you say?"

Reverend Short said nothing by way of response. Mr. Rutherford cast his eyes across the faces of the jury. There was nothing remarkable about them; they looked like the typical motley collection of housewives, labourers, bus drivers and retired accountants. A bald man on the far left appeared to be staring into space as if in a trance, and an attractive ginger-haired lady sitting next to him seemed to be far more interested in the state of her manicured fingernails than in the proper administration of criminal justice. They were plainly suffering from the Friday afternoon blues and needed to be stirred.

"Was that a question?" asked Reverend Short.

"Not really," responded Mr. Rutherford knowing full well that the inflexion in his voice had undoubtedly invited a reaction from Reverend Short. He would return to the subject in a moment but changed tack before doing so. "You are, of course a holy man, are you not, Reverend Short? A member of the clergy?"

"I am indeed," replied the Reverend. "I have been the vicar of my parish for the past thirty-six years."

"And you would, presumably, describe yourself as a devout Christian, would you not, Reverend Short?"

"I would most certainly describe myself as a devout Christian. I am a God-fearing man who does his best to do God's will. I strongly believe that we should adhere to the laws and principles laid down in the Holy Book. If more people did so, we could rid ourselves of the evils that plague modern society."

"I see," said Mr. Rutherford, pausing to consider his next question. "And what happened after you arrived at Miss Flowers' home? What did you do next, Reverend Short?"

"I parked my car, turned off the engine and, using the car's reading light, read to myself a couple of appropriate and relevant passages from the Bible – one from the Old and one from the New Testament."

"And for how long did you do this?"

"I think it must have been at least twenty minutes. You see, I had a clear view of Miss Flowers' house from where I was parked, and I wanted to be sure that she had gone to bed. I waited until all the lights had been switched off."

"And then?"

"Well, I waited another half an hour or so, by which time I assumed that Miss Flowers would be asleep. At what have must been close to half past eleven, I went to the front door carrying the container of petrol, which I then proceeded to pour through her letter box."

Reverend Short stopped at this critical part of the story and simply stared at Mr. Rutherford, as though his account of what happened was complete.

"You poured the petrol through the letter box. The whole gallon, presumably?"

"Yes."

"And then?" asked Mr. Rutherford, in a voice that indicated impatience and exasperation. "What then?"

"Well, then I lit a match, threw it inside the letter box and watched a fireball envelop the hall within seconds."

"You did this, presumably, with the clear intention of setting fire to the house whilst Miss Flowers was asleep, and with a view to killing her?"

"Yes, of course. Well, with the intention of burning her to death, to be more precise."

"Quite," responded Mr. Rutherford, again with a broad, disarming smile. "And you did this because you considered Miss Flowers to be a lady of the dark arts, a sorceress of some kind?"

"A witch, Mr. Rutherford. Let's not beat about the bush. She was a witch and, in order to follow the will of the Almighty, I could not permit her to live."

"You were obeying God's orders, were you, Reverend? You see, the problem I have with your course of conduct is this: when human beings wish to send a message to God, they normally do so in a socially accepted, rather harmless manner called praying. When human beings receive messages from God telling them to go forth and burn witches, that is not socially acceptable. In fact, it is often called paranoid schizophrenia. In this case, it is called murder. As a man of God, how can you possibly have thought that what you did was anything other than the commission of the most serious of crimes?"

"Mr. Rutherford," said Reverend Short. "My conscience is quite clear. I have adhered not only to the teachings of God but to the principles that underpin these proceedings. If you look at the plaque on the wall behind his Honour's chair, the coat of arms of this court bears four very plain Latin words: *Dieu et mon droit.* This translates to 'God and my right.' We are all here today by the grace of God, and to see that justice is done in the eyes of the Lord."

"I see your basic premise, Reverend, but I see nothing in this court room that promotes the idea that witches should be put to death."

"Oh no, Mr. Rutherford. You are quite wrong. Before giving my evidence today, I took an oath on the Holy Bible."

"And?"

"Perhaps I could take you to the relevant extract?"

Mr. Rutherford, for once at a loss for words, sighed and looked at the judge. "I am in your Lordship's hands."

The judge, with a weary look and a wave of his hand, responded with resignation. "Very well. Usher, please hand back to the Reverend the Bible on which he swore his oath."

The usher duly obliged and Reverend Short quickly thumbed through the book, beaming when he reached the page for which he had been looking.

"Ah, here it is. Exodus 22, verse 18. You shall not permit a witch to live. Could that be any clearer, Mr. Rutherford?"

"No, it could not. No further questions, my Lord."

THE LOVE

Tuesday the ninth of December was a workday like any other for Trevor Smith. He carefully parked his silver Audi in his usual spot at the far end of the station car park. He loved his usual spot and he was almost territorial about it, becoming annoyed if someone else occupied it. He liked certainty. After switching off his engine, Trevor picked up his battered leather briefcase and thick overcoat from the passenger seat, stepped out of the vehicle and pressed the remote control lock on his key fob. He trudged into the station and headed past the ticket machines, through the barrier towards the London bound platform that was starting to fill up with the usual array of other early risers. There were never more than thirty people or so at what his loving wife Nicole always called "that ungodly hour." Trevor did not think of it as an early start at all, even in the darkness of December. He rather liked it. As he settled down on a wooden bench near to where the front of the train stopped, Trevor quickly became lost in his own thoughts about a challenging meeting he had to attend that afternoon.

Trevor had been boarding the same 6.35am commuter train to Paddington for nearly twenty years. There had been precious little excitement over that two decade period. Some of the trains had been upgraded at the turn of the millennium; the timetable had shifted by two minutes or so at some stage in the long forgotten past and, about five years ago, someone in the carriage in front of Trevor's had suffered a fatal heart attack that caused the train to be delayed for more than an hour. That was about it. In general the whole network had become busier and more crowded, especially at peak times but, because of where he boarded, Trevor always managed to get a seat. On the whole, unforeseen disruption aside, he did not mind the trip too much. As a hardworking actuary for an insurance company in the City, Trevor usually buried himself in a work-related document for the duration of the fifty-minute journey, saving a novel or magazine for the return leg.

In the midst of his dull commute, there was only one minuscule, but very bright beacon of light that lifted Trevor's spirits no matter what the weather and however arduous or depressing the day ahead appeared to be. During all the years that Trevor had travelled into London, a woman of a similar age to Trevor, boarded the train at the next stop. Sometimes she sat near him. On occasion, she sat opposite him or next to him. Trevor had no idea who she was, what she did or what her name might be. They had never exchanged a word. The woman was never accompanied nor did she use a mobile phone on the train, so Trevor did not even know the sound of her voice. He had often wondered. She always wore a fashionable navy suit and the style of her dark brown hair was always the same – a beautifully cut bob that never seemed to alter in length or shade. Her black shoes were always polished to a sheen and they somehow seemed to pair perfectly with her piercing jet black eyes. Although on one level she looked severe, there was something about her face – perhaps her cheeks or her nose that somewhat softened the image. Maybe she was a lawyer or an investment banker. Trevor did not know and could do no more than guess. The only thing that Trevor did know about the woman was that to his mind, she was the most gorgeous creature on God's earth. Many years ago he wondered if he had grown obsessed by her. He was acutely aware that he always looked out for her and cheered up if she boarded his carriage. It was crazy really. Even now, if she sat next to him and happened to brush her arm or her leg against his, it sent a tiny tremor through his whole body that he could never quite control, much less rationalise.

As he sat down in his seat Trevor reached for his briefcase and fished out a slim file that he could quickly skim through in advance of his afternoon meeting. He put on his reading glasses, blew his nose and was soon annotating documents with a red pen. The woman boarded at the next stop and, although several other seats were available, she opted for the one opposite him. Trevor could feel his throat become dry. His spine stiffened. The woman produced a book from her briefcase and from the angle she held it, Trevor could just about see its title. Years of training in the art of self-restraint had taught Trevor that although he could comfortably look up and glance at the woman for a second, anything longer would quickly be perceived as staring. He had no intention of staring. Trevor attempted to concentrate on his file, but the words and figures seemed to float across his eyes. The simple truth was that he was hopelessly distracted, as he always was in the woman's presence. He may have been able to occupy his mind more easily if the woman's perfume had not wafted in his direction. It was always the same smell, but he knew nothing about perfume other than that his wife liked a classic brand which he dutifully bought each year for their anniversary. The woman's choice of fragrance was different – lighter and more flowery.

He wondered if she imagined, in any remote part of her brain, that the man sitting opposite her was savouring her perfume, choice of book and mere existence. He rather doubted it. He also wondered, as he often had before, if there existed a parallel universe in which he might have been married to this woman. One in which they shared a blissful life together with three gorgeous children. Not that he didn't love Nicole. He loved her deeply. He thought, as he had so often in the past, that his fantasy was simply an unexpressed frustration about Nicole's inability to have children. Or, perhaps it was the mental meanderings of a tragically dull actuary with so few highlights in his life that he needed to invent imaginary ones to relieve the monotony.

Just then, the train slowed down and then came to a halt. The driver announced that there would be a delay of a couple of minutes due to a red signal. Trevor could not help but sigh visibly and then shake his head. To his mind the fact that there was a red signal was not a reasonable explanation as to why the train needed to stop. If someone had thrown themselves in front of the train or if there was congestion due to an electrical failure with trains stacking up at the station ahead, that would be the beginning of an explanation. A red signal was a symptom, not a cause. Four minutes later the train was still static. Trevor could see that the woman was just as irritated by the delay as he was. She looked at her watch and let out what was plainly a grunt of dismay. For a fraction of a second, she glanced at Trevor. It was the sort of smile that spoke. It expressed a shared experience of early morning grumpiness and agitation. It expressed the sympathy born of joint suffering. Trevor responded with an identical smile, but then quickly returned his gaze to his file, albeit that he had no intention of reading it.   After another minute or two, the train made a stuttering attempt to continue on its course towards Paddington, gradually accelerating until it returned to a proper speed.

The rest of the journey took place without incident and the train slowed down shortly before half past seven as it made its final approach into Paddington. Trevor looked out of the window. The wintery half light was hazy and insipid. Several passengers made their way in clusters towards the doors. Trevor and the woman remained seated. Trevor wondered if she was so gripped by her novel that she had failed to notice that the train had nearly arrived at the terminus. As it finally came to a halt, Trevor and the woman found themselves to be the only passengers still seated. Seconds passed but neither Trevor nor the woman moved. A few moments later she closed her book and looked up. She looked at Trevor and with an impulse that came from the innermost depths of his heart Trevor moved his lips. As he spoke he felt as though he was having an out of body experience. Someone else was moving his vocal cords. Not him.

"I love you," he professed, staring into the woman's deep dark eyes.

In the nanosecond that followed Trevor prepared his cheek for a violent slap and a few stinging words of invective. He winced and braced himself. The blow, when it came, was devastating – far more devastating.

"And I love you," replied the woman.

Angela

"You can take that look off your face for starters, Angela," Brian said with an aggrieved tone to his voice. "It's the sort of self-satisfied smirk that really makes me angry. Please stop it. You were so charming and engaging when I first met you. What happened? You would never have dreamt of giving anyone that kind of filthy stare, least of all me. Just stop it."

Brian moved across the kitchen to the sink, in which sat a yellow plastic bucket, filled with soapy water and a number of dirty utensils. Deep amber sunlight slanted down at a low angle through the kitchen window, catching the bubbles on the foamy surface of the bucket. Brian put on his marigold gloves and his pinafore. He then meticulously scrubbed each item before placing them, one by one, on the sideboard to dry.

"I can recall so vividly the first time I saw you. It was a really hot, sunny day last July, and you were coming out of college with your three friends. Or was it August? I think one was called Lucy – the one with the bright red flowery frock. And what was the name of the other one? The one with the auburn hair?" Angela said nothing. "I think her name was Charlotte. Yes, I'm sure it was. Charlotte. You all skipped out of college on what I think was your last day of term. You were so happy then. Oops, forgive me. That's the front door."

Having heard the chime of his doorbell, Brian quickly removed his rubber gloves and headed to the front door, gently closing the kitchen door behind him. The doorbell chimed a second time before Brian had time to open it.

"Alright, alright, I'm coming," shouted Brian. "Give me a second." He arrived at the front door and opened it, gingerly at first but fully when he recognised the familiar face of his neighbour. "Hello, Mrs. Rogers," said Brian cheerfully. "What can I do for you?"

"Hello, Brian," answered Mrs. Rogers, wincing enough as she spoke to suggest that a request would soon follow. It usually did. "I'm so sorry to disturb you, but it's about Fender. He hasn't been seen for days."

"Fender?" asked Brian blankly, appearing somewhat distracted.

"Fender. My lovely cat Fender, of course. You know. I mentioned it to you yesterday. The last I saw of him was in the garden last Wednesday and he seems to have vanished into thin air. It's so unlike him. Have you seen him, Brian? You're always at home, so I thought maybe you had."

"No, I'm afraid I haven't, Mrs. Rogers. I'm so sorry. What does he look like?"

"Oh, you know Fender, Brian. He's black with deep green eyes and a white patch over his left eye."

"Well, you do have five other cats, Mrs. Rogers. I'm afraid that I rather lose track. And so do you, it seems."

"If you do see him, you will let me know immediately, won't you? You will keep an eye out? I don't know," added Mrs. Rogers with a sigh, "there are some odd people about. Someone may have stolen him. Or kidnapped him!"

"I don't think that's very likely, Mrs. Rogers. I'm sure he'll turn up sooner or later. Now, if you'll excuse me," said Brian, with a flick of his head, indicating that he had things to get on with.

"Oh, I'm sorry, Brian. I didn't realise you had company. I'll leave you to it, but do look out for Fender. You will, won't you?"

Brian issued a broad, rather forced smile that made it clear there was nothing left to say as he gently closed the door. Through the round translucent multi-coloured window at the top of the door, Brian could see Mrs. Rogers hovering on the porch for several seconds after he closed the door. It was as if she wanted to say more, though Brian made it very plain that he was not interested in the case of the missing cat. He stared at the front door until it was clear that Mrs. Rogers had departed. He then returned to the kitchen.

"I'm so sorry about that, Angela. It was Mrs. Roger's from next door. She's very tiresome. She always drops in on me when she has a problem. Last week she was asking me about her lumbago. I mean, what do I know about lumbago?"

At that moment the telephone rang. "Forgive me, but it's probably Mother, so I'd better get it."

Brian scurried to the hall, where a plastic green telephone sat on a little table with a seat next to it.

"Edmonton four-one-eight-one," said Brian in his best telephone voice. "Oh, Mother, it's you," he said, his voice reverting to its South London twang. "I thought it might be. How are you? I'm fine, too. I'm sorry I haven't been over to see you this week, but I've just been so busy with one thing and another. You know how it is. Hobbies can be so absorbing and time-consuming that you almost forget everything else. I don't know where the days go sometimes. How's your rheumatism? Oh good, I'm so glad to hear that. And is everything okay with Doris? You mentioned that she has been rather poorly. Oh good, I'm glad to hear that, too." Glancing at his watch, Brian suddenly realised the time. It was a quarter to five and the hardware shop would soon be closing.

"Sorry to cut you short, Mother, but I have just realised that the hardware shop shuts in a quarter of an hour and I need to pick up some saw-dust and other supplies that I ordered last week. I'd like to get there before it closes. Look after yourself and we'll speak tomorrow. Bye-bye." Brian quickly donned his overcoat, hat and shoes, shouting loudly as he turned to exit the house. "I've got to pop out, Angela. I'll be back in half an hour or so. Apologies. It's for your benefit."

Brian scurried along his suburban road toward the small hardware store, a corner shop that was no more than a five minute walk. The owner, Mr. Wedlake, knew Brian well, as he was a good customer.

"Hello, Brian," said Mr. Wedlake with a grin as Brian entered the shop. "How are you? I was going to call and remind you that everything you ordered is in. You are so reliable that I was surprised you didn't come yesterday. I assumed you were busy."

"I'm fine, thanks. I was indeed busy. Very busy."

"No problem at all, Brian," said Mr. Wedlake, handing a large cardboard box of materials over the counter. "Will you be alright with all that lot? It's a rather heavy load, I'm afraid. I could drop you at your house in my van after I close, if you like?"

"Not to worry. That won't be necessary. I'll manage. How much will that be?"

"Er... it comes to one pound, one shilling and six pence. Just over a guinea," replied Mr. Wedlake. Brian reached for his wallet. "Oh, don't worry about payment now, Brian. I'll put it on your account. Many thanks."

"Thank you," said Brian, struggling with the box as he opened the shop door with his elbow. Brian trudged back towards his house. It was just starting to rain a little, and although the contents of the box were well-covered, it was clear that if anything got damp it would be disastrous, so he shielded the top of the box with his body and quickened his pace.

"Home, Angela!" he shouted as he entered the house. He put down the box, carefully hung up his coat and hat and then picked up the box again before returning to the kitchen. "I'll make a nice cup of tea and then we can get to work," said

Brian. "I need a pick-me-up after that journey back from the hardware shop. I feel rather exhausted what with one thing and another."

He put the kettle on the gas stove, scooped two tea-spoons of tea into his tea-pot and reached for his favourite china cup and saucer from the cupboard next to the sink. After refreshing himself with tea and a shortbread biscuit, Brian scrubbed his hands under the tap and set to work preparing the taxidermic materials that would allow him to put the finishing touches to Angela's head. The lips and eyes were always tricky, so it was probably going to be a long night. He carefully placed the head on the kitchen table. After pushing his hacksaw to one side, he set to work. He then looked up at the stuffed body of Fender, perched stock still on the kitchen shelf above him, with his plastic green eyes glinting in the fluorescent light. The eyes seemed to watch him, so Brian tilted the body slightly. It wouldn't make too much difference if Fender stared out towards the garden. Perhaps he would do the same with Angela.

Down the Tube

Pippa glanced down wearily at her watch. It was much later than she thought.

"Chris, I'm really sorry, but I simply have to leave. I'll miss the last train if I don't," she said softly, with an aching desire not to leave at all. Pippa drained the final few drops of white wine from her glass and reached for her handbag, fumbling as she attempted to close it properly. The Queen's Head was now devoid of any customers, although Pippa and Chris had been so absorbed in their own company that they had barely noticed. The pub manager stopped the music and dimmed the lights, a clear hint that it was time to go.

"Do you absolutely have to? I'd much prefer it if you stay at my place. I'll really miss you. I honestly will," Chris responded with a childish grin.

Pippa steepled her fingers on the table and pushed her glass and beer mat to one side as she did. She paused and stared into Chris's delicious blue eyes for several seconds without saying a word. She exhaled gently and smiled in a teasing fashion.

"Tomorrow night," she whispered. "I've already explained. I have got to be up at the crack of dawn in the morning to get to work in time for our bloody breakfast team-building meeting. It'll be deadly dull, but I need to play the part and be there on time. All my stuff is at home. I'm sorry. I really am." Pippa reached for Chris's hand and placed hers on top of his, squeezing gently and then harder for a moment before releasing it.

"I do understand, but I don't think you should go on the tube on your own late at night. It's not at all safe for anyone who is on their own. Think about the stabbing that took place at Tufnell Park tube a few months ago. It was in the papers."

"I'll be fine. The trains are never empty nowadays, even late at night," said Pippa. "I'll be okay. You don't need to worry about me."

"Well, the least I can do is walk you to the station," said Chris. "I hope you'll permit me that honour?"

Pippa nodded and the young couple donned their heavy winter overcoats and headed for the exit. It was bitterly cold outside and Pippa immediately linked arms with Chris, huddling next to him for comfort and warmth. She was starting to regret her fourth drink of the evening, but the time had sped by so effortlessly that she had hardly bothered to keep track. The streets were deserted, the cars parked alongside the road to the station were all coated in frost that glistened under the street lamps and the sky was an inky black colour, spoilt only by a faint wash of orange light pollution. They did not speak to each other as they walked along. Neither of them felt the need – the afterglow from a lovely evening was enough.

After five minutes or so, they reached the entrance to the tube station, wherePippa broke the silence.

"I'll be fine from here," she said, kissing Chris firmly on the lips before turning on her heels to depart.

"Are you sure you don't want to come back to my place?" asked Chris. Pippa turned and watched Chris screw up his face in a final non-verbal plea. Pippa responded with a forced smile and turned towards the station entrance.

As she entered the station, Pippa remembered that her oyster card needed topping up. She had meant to do it earlier in the day. She looked at her watch again and realised that she needed to get a move on. Otherwise, despite her best efforts, she would either end up back at Chris's house or be forced to splash out forty pounds on a cab. She stepped up to the machine on the wall and rummaged around in her handbag. She panicked momentarily when she could not immediately find her oyster card, but it was eventually unearthed from inside her paperback where it had become wedged. She swiftly topped it up. As she was paying, Pippa had the odd sensation that someone was watching her from behind. She turned around, but saw no one. The truth was, despite her bravado with Chris, tube stations late at night were often empty and they gave her the creeps. Pippa steeled her nerves and told herself to stop imagining things. She looked at her watch again, forgetting that she had done so only a minute or so earlier. Her mild overindulgence was taking its toll.

Pippa hurried through the barrier and towards the down escalator. She stood on the escalator for a few seconds, but then decided to skip down at a reasonable pace. Again, she had a sixth sense that someone was behind her, watching or following her, but she looked all around and there was absolutely no one to be seen. No staff, no passengers – no one. After stepping off the escalator, Pippa headed down a long, brightly-lit tunnel that took her in the direction of the northbound Bakerloo Line. As she turned the first corner, she stopped briefly in her tracks where she was unexpectedly confronted by a tramp lying spread-eagled on the floor. His face was beetroot red, his teeth were yellow and protruding like those of an oversized rat and he was draped in a greasy brown coat. Although the empty can of super-strength lager lying next to him suggested that he was drunk, the tramp lay utterly motionless with one eye open, as if he were dead. Whatever his state, Pippa quickly decided to ignore him and move on.

A hundred metres further on, Pippa heard a disturbing noise. It was an odd banging sound that seemed out of place in a tube station. For a second or two Pippa was gripped by an icy fear. She quickened her pace and sped up even more as she heard the sound of a train arriving at the platform just around the corner and down a short flight of stairs. Pippa dashed as fast as she could as she heard the train's engine stop. As she clattered down the last step she could clearly make out the beeping sound that preceded the closing of the doors. As she came out onto the platform, she hurled herself towards the nearest double door of the train just as it closed. Having failed to board by a second or so, she swore at herself, cursing her earlier dawdling. She panted heavily. The illuminated train indicator stated that the next train would be along in ten minutes, which was fine but she knew the wait could cause her to miss the last train out of Baker Street where she had to change.

Pippa slumped down on a bench. She was still out of breath and sweating, so she tried to compose herself. There was no one else on the platform. The banging noise had abated, but she still felt ill at ease. She tried to cast all bad thoughts from her mind, but was unable to distract herself, so she started fiddling with her bag. Just as Pippa began to calm down, she heard another sound. It was the distinct sound of footsteps, following her very route and heading towards the platform. Animal instinct took over and Pippa knew she should not stay put. She rushed along the platform towards an exit leading to the southbound platform. She scurried out of sight and waited with her back to the wall in an adjacent corridor. Although the person was probably more than thirty metres away, she could hear a man swearing under his breath. Pippa remained fixed to the spot. She then heard the heavy footsteps again, moving along the platform in her direction. As the sound approached, she decided to make a run for it, but as soon as she launched into a sprint she heard the clatter of the footsteps behind her doing precisely the same. Pippa dashed like a lunatic up another short flight of stairs towards a tunnel on the left. Although she was fast, the footsteps behind her were faster, and just as she turned the corner into the tunnel she heard yelling behind her.

"Pippa, for Christ sake, stop running! Where the hell are you going?" It was Chris, who struggled to catch his breath.

"Where am I going?" shouted Pippa at the top of her voice, repeating his question. "What in the name of God are you doing here chasing me? You scared the life out of me!"

Chris paused with comic timing. He grinned and reached for his trouser pocket.

"You forgot these," he said, dangling Pippa's house keys in front of his eyes like a hypnotist.

THE NEW ARRIVAL

It was Sunday 7th October 1900, the Sabbath. A cold and blustery autumnal wind buffeted the windows, but it was warm and cosy indoors. Anna had done a truly marvellous job preparing for the arrival of their new baby. He was proud of her. She had completely transformed the box room into a beautiful nursery. They had not had enough money to decorate when Gebhard was born two years earlier and although they were still not flush with money, they both decided to employ the services of a professional decorator to repaint the walls and ceiling in order to get the job done properly. It looked and smelt wonderful. Anna applied a number of motherly finishing touches that made the room particularly attractive and homely. She made up the colourful curtains with fine linen and created the decorated pelmet that rounded off the windows nicely.

With a little help from a friend, she made an intricate white crochet bed cover that she carefully placed in position. It was also Anna's hard work and knitting skills that produced a white baby suit together with sweet, tiny booties that she positioned on display on a table in the corner of the room. A stickler for detail, she placed a teddy bear next to the baby's pillow, a toy that had become curiously fashionable amongst local mothers over the years. One of her friends at church had kindly given it to her when Gebhard was born and, because he was such a bonny healthy boy, she regarded the worn, soft creature as something of a good luck charm, the benefit of which could be passed along to her next child. The wooden crib was not new, but it could be used again, as it was only two years old and in impeccable condition. Gebhard had outgrown it, but she had both an emotional and practical attachment to it, not least of all because it was a wonderful device for rocking a small baby to sleep.

Anna's husband spent the early part of that Sunday at the hospital, pacing up and down the hall, smoking cigarettes and trying unsuccessfully to distract himself. Unfortunately, he found this extremely difficult, as he was a born worrier. Although not a devout Roman Catholic like his wife, he prayed that everything would go as smoothly as it had with their first-born. There were so many cases of infant mortality or mothers dying during childbirth that it was hard not to foster black fears in the darker recesses of his mind.

The outing to the hospital had turned out to be a false alarm so he and Anna returned home, preferring the comfort of familiar surroundings to the harsh environment of the maternity ward. When her contractions started again at lunchtime, he called for the doctor, who appeared with characteristic speed and enthusiasm. He was a bald-headed portly chap who had been the family's trusted medical adviser for years. He did not claim to be a specialist in childbirth, or anything else for that matter, but he instilled confidence and was certainly experienced in a broad range of procedures. Anna's sister also turned up to help. She was a rather dim-witted sickly creature, but she was well-intentioned and if Anna welcomed her presence then he would not dream of interfering. He could do nothing more than step back and hope everything ended well.

From his position in his armchair in the living room, he could clearly hear Anna's cries of pain in the bedroom above. He wondered why God imposed the terrible pain of childbirth on women, when the whole process was supposed to be natural. Surely someone, given the advanced technologies of the new century, could devise a way of making the ordeal safer and less painful. Anna had suffered enough during both pregnancies with morning sickness and high blood pressure. Was there a dreadful divine plan to deprive Anna of respite? It simply wasn't fair.

By late afternoon the sky had darkened, but there was no evidence of progress upstairs. The doctor had come down an hour earlier to say that Anna's spirits remained high and that he had administered some laudanum to calm her nerves. He assured him that with God on Anna's side, all would be fine and he was very confident of a happy outcome for mother and child.

By this stage, he felt a strong need to calm his nerves with his favourite pipe tobacco and a stiff schnapps. The wind outside was howling and black thunderclouds suggested that a ferocious storm was imminent. There was no question of returning to the hospital. Suddenly, he heard a rumble from above. A thunderclap seemed to herald the arrival of his new child and indeed, the noise from the heavens was quickly followed by the sound of scurrying footsteps and a flurry of activity.

The storm ensued and soon the windows were battered by powerful sheets of rain. Curling brown leaves from the linden trees outside were ripped from their branches and hurled in violent eddies. The odd streak of lightning electrified the scene, adding to the drama. Cocooned in his living room, the storm simply added to his fear and unease. He briefly contemplated going upstairs to see what was going on, but he soon dismissed the notion as foolhardy. He could be of no assistance, and it would do no more than satisfy his curiosity. He slumped back in his armchair again and waited. Half an hour later, Anna's sister came downstairs to fetch more water and towels.

"Anna is doing very well but is extremely fatigued," she said quickly. "I am sure that it is only a matter of minutes now. If you'll forgive me..."

"Of course, of course. Please don't let me hold you up. I am sure you are doing everything you can."

After another agonising forty-five minutes, the doctor clattered downstairs and headed for the living room. He wore a bloodstained apron that made him look more like a butcher than a doctor.

The doctor had removed his tie and rolled up his sleeves. The lines and perspiration on his brow told their own story but, more importantly, so did his beaming smile. In his arms he cradled a baby, whose reddened face was barely visible from underneath a chunky, lily-white shawl.

"I am pleased to announce that you are the father to a second son! Please accept my heartiest congratulations to you and your charming wife."

"What wonderful, joyous news! Thank you so much for your professional help and your loyalty to this family. You are a true friend." He then took the baby in his arms and stared into his stunningly blue eyes. The sight of the baby's cherub-like cheeks and perfect rosebud lips made him well up with tears of pride and joy. "What a beautiful boy! I am so proud. Thank you again." He rocked his newborn son for a moment before handing the small bundle back to the doctor. He then rushed upstairs to the bedroom, where his wife was being tended to by her sister, who used a damp flannel to cool her forehead.

"Darling," he shouted, "you are a marvel! You have given us a second son. I am so proud I don't know what to say. He is gorgeous and so are you." He went to her side and hugged her with open arms. She was too feeble to respond in kind but she grinned broadly.

"We must thank our Lord," she said, placing her left hand on the beautifully-bound leather bible she kept at her bedside. "He has blessed us with this gift and we should be grateful for our good fortune. We must pray that our son will follow the path of righteousness and good, and that he and his brother will grow to be devout Christian citizens."

Having cleaned himself up and removed his apron, the doctor returned to the bedroom, where he rolled down his sleeves and began to put his tie back on.

"My work here is done. I will bid you farewell and will return tomorrow morning." Donning his coat, he threw a final glance towards Anna. "Have you thought of a name for the baby yet, Frau Himmler?"

"Not yet," she replied. "I quite like the name Hans, which I am told means 'gift from God,' but my husband is not so sure. We'll think of something."

The Homecoming

Philip Rochester had wondered what this day would be like for more than twenty-five years. Now that it had finally arrived, he could hardly believe it.

He was intensely irritated that smoking appeared to be prohibited just about everywhere; his last nicotine fix had been hours ago and he needed another one badly. His eyes surveyed the carriage, where almost everyone in sight fiddled with a mobile phone or electronic device and this grated on him too. He felt different and out of place, as he possessed no such gadgets. He was sure that when they looked up from their gizmos, one or two of his fellow passengers had been staring at him. They could probably sense something odd about him, something that made him an outsider. A huddle of young girls seated at the far end of the carriage giggled amongst themselves. One of them caught his eye and flashed him a look that made it clear she regarded him as some kind of nutter. He immediately dropped his head and turned to face the window, looking at the dreary urban landscape as it whizzed past. He fidgeted self-consciously with his right earlobe and tried to suppress the ruddy blush that prickled under his skin. He was uncomfortable and it showed.

As the train pulled hesitantly into Liverpool Street Station, Philip reached for his compact travel bag and placed it on his lap. He glanced around warily as the other passengers gathered their belongings and headed for the doors. The station looked different to how he remembered it, but Philip struggled to recall precisely what had changed. It seemed bigger, though he wondered if his mind had distorted certain images after all these years. It was definitely more crowded, but it was also much brighter and cleaner. After everyone had alighted from the carriage, Philip finally did the same. He shuffled along the platform, looking from side to side every now and again. He handed in his ticket at the barrier and walked towards the new and modern station concourse.

Philip had long ago decided on his first port of call. He went straight to the entrance to the tube where he purchased a ticket to Arnos Grove on the Piccadilly Line. He recalled that this leg of his journey was an easy one with one change at Kings Cross. He ambled towards the escalator and proceeded on his way, emerging at the suburban outpost of Arnos Grove an hour later. From there he could have travelled onwards by bus or taxi, but he elected to walk. He was savouring every moment of being back in England and even found pleasure in the trudge through the suburbs on a chilly October day. It was a pleasant change from the monotony of incessant sunshine and deep blue skies that he had endured for so long.

Fifteen minutes later, he had arrived at the New Southgate Cemetery, which he entered through two black wrought-iron gates. A small office near the entrance was positioned to one side and shaded by a tall oak tree that, despite the autumnal elements, still clung to the bulk of its leaves. Philip entered the office, where he encountered an elderly man with leathery skin and tiny, piggy eyes. The man smiled at him weakly from the other side of a counter.

"Can I help you?" he asked.

"Yes, I wonder if you would. I'm looking for two graves in the name of Rochester. I assume you have a register and a plan to help me find them?"

"Yes indeed, sir," replied the man with a gravelly voice. "If you happen to know the dates of death that would be most helpful."

Philip recounted the relevant dates as the man fetched the register, a dusty, old tome that seemed to be bound in the same coarse material as the man's skin. Philip sat on a chair and began thumbing through the pages. When he was armed with the numbers of the two graves and a plan that comprised of three A4 sheets stapled together, Philip made his way across a series of broken tarmac paths to the first grave. The headstone was new and in perfect condition. It bore the name of his wife, Rose Rochester, the date of her death three months earlier and a brief inscription. Philip took a deep breath. He had imagined shedding a tear at this point, but he did not. Their time together had been too long ago. He often wondered why Rose had never remarried. She had not even bothered to revert to her maiden name.

After consulting the plan, he trudged over to a different part of the grounds that was obviously less well maintained. Most of the tombstones in this section were weather-beaten and old. He finally reached the end of row H227 where he saw for the first time his own tombstone. Dark velvety moss and yellowy green lichen obscured the inscription, but his name was still clearly legible. He chuckled to himself and smiled wryly thinking there couldn't be many people who saw their own tombstone. He cast a brief look up to the heavens before turning on his heels towards the exit.

The next leg of his journey was of equally little practical consequence. He hopped on the number 34 double-decker bus and off again several stops later. He imagined that the people around him were still watching him. The bus driver had certainly given him an odd look as he boarded, even though his behaviour was completely unremarkable. As the bus retreated into the distance, Philip felt certain that an ugly middle-aged woman with a cadaverous face was peering at him from a top window near the rear of the bus. He moved on with haste.

Philip walked the length of the road on which he had lived all his adult life, before his untimely departure. His former home was a typical semi-detached mock Tudor house built in the 1930's. It appeared tired now, and would require more than a lick of paint to be restored to its former glory. Happy memories of long, hot summers and snowy winters came flooding back. He stared up at one of the bedroom windows and noticed a twitch from behind one of the net curtains. He walked down the road to another house just a stone's throw away. It was the one in which he had spent his childhood. It was of similar construction and even more dilapidated than the house he'd just visited. It looked as though it had been empty for some time. With curiosity and pangs of nostalgia behind him, Philip knew that he no longer needed to kill time. He had more important matters to tend to.

Philip arrived at the bank just before 2pm.

"Hello," he said to a young assistant at the counter. "I'm here for a two o'clock appointment with Mr. Fuller."

"Certainly, sir. If you would be so kind as to wait here, Mr. Fuller will collect you in a moment. I'll tell him you are here." Mr. Fuller duly arrived within a couple of minutes and escorted Philip into a Spartan meeting room kitted out with little more than with two chairs, a desk and a computer screen. Hardly the Rolls-Royce treatment for one of your wealthiest clients, thought Philip. Mr. Fuller seemed sheepish before he spoke. He didn't look Philip in the eye, which was disconcerting.

"Well, thank you for coming in, Mr. Collins," said Mr. Fuller. "I'm sorry to trouble you with the inconvenience of meeting here, but I'm afraid I have to follow the bank's procedures, especially where large sums of money are concerned."

"I quite understand," said Philip.

"I appreciate that you wanted to deal with this matter remotely, via your bank abroad, but the account of FPS Financial Group contains in excess of ten million pounds, with accrued interest, and has been dormant now for nearly twenty—seven years. My compliance people simply wouldn't allow me to deal with your request to transfer the money, even though all of the paperwork is in order and you are, of course, the proper signatory. You know what sticklers for detail they are. They wanted me to meet you in person. 'Know-your-client,' and all that."

"I fully appreciate their concerns," replied Philip, not wishing to say much more. "Anyway, I brought my passport, as you requested," he added, handing over the fake document that he had had made several months earlier. Mr. Fuller looked at it briefly, smiled and started clicking on the keyboard of his computer. Philip started to feel more comfortable. He told himself long ago that he was much smarter than the everyday fraudster who quietly slips out of the country without getting caught. He was better than that. He was dead. He did not exist. Indeed, there was no one left in England who could recognise him. Although returning would be safe, Philip had never dared to take the chance until now. His money had run out and he had gambling debts and other expenses in Northern Cyprus. It was simply too upsetting to think of his money languishing in an English bank account, unused, only earning tuppence ha'penny in interest. He needed it. He had to get his hands on it. Then he could disappear back into his quiet life in the sun without anyone knowing the difference.

"Well, everything seems to be perfectly in order, Mr. Collins," said Mr. Fuller. "We should be able to transfer the money first thing in the morning." He made two further clicks on his computer before standing. Philip was about to do the same when Mr. Fuller spoke again. "If you'll just wait here a second, Mr. Collins, my colleague will join us shortly."

Philip frowned. He was perplexed by the delay. A moment later the grey shape of a tall man appeared on the other side of the frosted glass door to the room. The door inched open and an imposing figure in a suit appeared. He was in his late fifties and had the square jaw of a rugby player.

"Hello," said the man as he entered the room with a smile. "Mr. Rochester, I presume? Mr. Philip Rochester?" Philip was too stunned to speak, but his flushed scarlet face revealed everything. "My name is Andrews," the man said. "Detective Inspector Andrews. I've wondered what this day would be like for more than twenty-five years. Now that it's finally arrived I can hardly believe it."

The Blast from the Past

A shudder went through him. It was her. Jennifer Whittle. He was sure of it. Of course she had changed in twenty years, but it was her alright. Jennifer Whittle, the girl about whom every boy in class had obsessed during their teenage years. Jennifer Whittle, the untouchable one. Back in the eighties he would have given his right arm for an evening out with her. All of the boys would have done so, without exception, though none did, because no one would take the chance. There was lots of chit-chat about her long-standing boyfriend, but no one had even met him. There was, to use the terminology used by his old chemistry teacher, Mr. Foster, no empirical evidence. There was no proof that a boyfriend existed, but even if he didn't, he still served a purpose. He gave all of the boys an excuse not to ask Jennifer out. The real reason none dared to do so was because she was, to put it bluntly, a goddess. It would have been impossible to go to the cinema or a restaurant with an unearthly, ethereal legend like Jennifer. You could do that with her best friend Julie, and many had, but not with Jennifer. That was fanciful. The stuff of dreams.

There was something about the way she stood that gave it away in an instant – she often crossed her legs while standing and cocked her head to the side when conversing. Her hair was the same golden blonde colour, although he guessed it now came from a bottle. It still bore the same textural hallmarks – wavy, shiny and very full, although it was slightly shorter now. Shoulder-length would not have looked quite right on her now that she was in her late thirties but the adjustment was good. No, it was better than good. It was perfect. Even at this distance, some fifteen metres or so, he could see that her teeth were still like white pearls and her thin lips still smiled in the same way they always had, with a slight curl, a hint of a grin, a suggestion of wickedness. Unlike so many of her peers with whom he had kept in touch and who had already gone to seed, Jennifer had clearly managed to maintain her figure. She was still stunning. It went without saying that Jennifer, being the celestial creature she was, had what one could only describe as a heavenly body. She still did. It wasn't just that she was beautifully-proportioned; she had the sort of poise you'd normally associate with a ballerina or gymnast. Not that she had been particularly sporty, although he suddenly had a vivid recollection of Jennifer playing for the netball team. He recalled the girls' Head of Games, Miss Hill, being irritated by the huge crowd of boys that turned up to watch the school netball matches when Jennifer was playing. It annoyed Miss Hill because she wanted the pupils to cheer on the entire team, but the boys were not there to do anything of the kind of the kind. They just wanted to watch Jennifer in her netball kit as she flitted around the court, nymph-like. Their interest in netball was no greater than their interest in geometry. Other than, of course, the geometry of Jennifer Whittle, a source of endless talk and fantasy.

Jennifer Whittle's unexpected reappearance had lit up, if not completely transformed, what would otherwise have been a very dull drinking session. It had been a bugger of a day for Mike, who spent most of his waking hours staring at a screen of commodities prices bathed in red. He was under severe pressure to make budget before year-end but there was little volume in the products his group traded in, and without a bull market or even a flicker of real activity, there was precious little chance of making up lost ground. It wasn't just losing his bonus that bothered him; he could soon find that his job was in jeopardy. His employers, the subsidiary of a huge California asset management company, would show little sympathy if his figures were lousy. Greg, his closest work colleague had persuaded him, against his will and under duress, to join him after work for a swift glass of "something filthy" at a wine bar on the corner of Lombard Street. The previous night had also been a late one, spent entertaining some crazy Japanese clients who made him drink industrial quantities of sake until the early hours of the morning. The last thing Mike needed was more alcohol and another late night. If he carried on at this rate, he'd need a new liver by Christmas. He'd nevertheless decided to keep Greg company at the wine bar for no more than an hour, after which he would slope off and leave. At least that was the plan before he spotted Jennifer Whittle. He wasn't quite so sure now. Even after all this time it was obvious to Mike that Jennifer's magnetic aura had not lost its spellbinding potency. It was irrational, but he couldn't bear to ignore her and walk away, never to see her again. He wanted to capture this new memory of her, if only in his brain.

Greg prattled on about last night's football match – a grim encounter between his team, West Ham, and Blackburn, their relegation zone rivals. Because Greg already had three vodka-based drinks under his belt, he seemed completely unaware of Mike's lack of engagement in their typical banter. Mike, on the other hand, was acutely aware that he was not in the mood for football talk. He could not help but peek across the bar towards Jennifer, who was steadfastly ensconced in conversation with a swaggering sharp-suited city bloke ten years younger than her. He was precisely the kind of Adonis that Mike would never be, with a flop of brown hair neatly gelled into position, a stripy pink shirt, loud tie and stupidly oversized cufflinks. There was a look of lust on his face that Jennifer shamelessly encouraged. Bored with any further discussion of the West Ham players' lack of shooting prowess, Mike decided to reveal his thoughts to Greg.

"Greg, mate. You see the girl over there by the window?"

"The blonde?"

"Yeah. The looker talking to the short bloke with braces who looks like something out of a bad remake of Wall Street."

"I see her. What about her?"

"I was at school with her twenty years ago. She was the pin-up girl of our year. Still looks pretty good. Jennifer Whittle is her name. She was undoubtedly most gorgeous creature to ever walk the earth. Well, at least that's how it seemed at the time."

"I assume you gave her one, you dirty rascal," said Greg crudely.

"Christ, no. Not Jennifer. You don't understand. She was a divine being, a demigoddess well beyond the reach of mere mortals, let alone the spotty nerd I was."

"And still are," added Greg, unable to resist the quip.

"No one in our year ever got near her. The closest I got was sitting next to her on the coach on a geography field trip to Wales. I don't think that counts as consummating a sexual relationship, do you?" Greg laughed and slapped Mike on the back.

"I'm just off for a slash," said Greg. "One for the road after that? Then I'll let you go home to your slippers, your Horlicks and your dreams about the delectable Jennifer."

"Sure," replied Mike, distracted again. "Same again?" he asked as he turned towards the bar, not waiting for a response from his drinking companion. He shuffled through the crowd of merry drinkers with an eye on Jennifer, who still seemed engrossed in deep conversation with her young, Michael Douglas lookalike. The idea that he should steel himself to say something had formed within half a second of seeing her. It was not going to go away now. The question was whether he actually had the guts to do it. Could he put the inhibitions of yesteryear behind him and confidently do that which he had never been able to do as a callow youth? Would Jennifer cast a spell on him and turn him into a frog if he dared to speak to her? Surely not, but what would be the point? She probably wouldn't remember him anyway.

Whilst pondering what to do, Mike resolved to fortify himself with some Dutch courage by ordering two "large ones" of the same poison in which he and Greg had already overindulged. After several big glugs and a quick word in Greg's ear, Mike decided to do the unthinkable and speak to Jennifer, if only to say hello. If she remembered him it would be enough. He'd be chuffed and would know that he'd finally put to bed the childish fear that she might bite his head off.

As he moved towards her, the memories came flooding back with more brilliant intensity. Closer up, she was just as beautiful as she had always been. She was still the most radiant female he had ever encountered. Once he stood right next to her, he had left himself with no choice. The words caught in his throat, but he managed to speak normally.

"Hi, I'm really sorry to interrupt. I'm sure you won't remember me, but I was in your class at school. I'm Mike. Mike Reynolds."

Jennifer's male friend scowled at him with eyes that pierced through him like high-velocity bullets, though he said nothing. Jennifer looked perplexed, if not deeply mystified, but certainly not hostile.

"I'm so sorry, Mike. I'm pleased to meet you, but I'm afraid I don't remember you from Orpington High," she replied.

The penny dropped, suddenly and with force.

"Orpington High?" asked Mike. "You're not Jennifer Whittle, are you?" he added with a mixture of mirth and relief.

"No, I'm not," she replied with the sort of smile that would melt anyone's heart.

THE JOURNEY

Straight ahead of him was more of the same. It had been like this for as long as he could remember. It was endless. A chaotic circus of gigantic, moist leaves confronted him, followed by wall after wall of tangled, snarling interwoven trunks and branches, straggling willowy creepers, bushes, thickets and fronds. He was ensnared by an overwhelming web of greenery, and it seemed as though his only way out was to hack his way through. He stumbled on, desperately whacking the overgrown foliage with the serrated blade of his huge machete.

The dingy air was abuzz with swarms of flying creatures – great and small, beautiful and ugly – lemon hornets, shiny jade dragonflies, magenta butterflies, gnats and flies of varying shapes and proportions. The thick atmosphere was so clogged with tiny bugs it was hard to breathe without choking on the wretched insects. There were birds, too – orange-breasted trogans, toucans, scarlet lorikeets, macaws, bushy-crested hornbills, scrubfowls and parakeets. All of them seemed to squawk and yawp tirelessly at maximum volume. The multitudinous flying creatures were more than matched in number by their counterparts on the ground, slippery slugs, soft-bodied termites, hard-bodied arthropods, red ants, black ants, white ants. Everything squelched underfoot as he waded through a damp carpet of crushed vegetation. His body was drenched in sweat and brown filth and his soggy clothes clung to him, rubbing against his sore legs and irritating the scratches and swellings on his arms and face.

Periodically, the leafy canopy arching above him would thin out enough to reveal small patches of sky. The firmament mostly comprised of tormented, greyish-purple clouds and rain, but on this occasion it was bright blue, and slices of the sun's rays cut through the trees and plants, illuminating parts of the bedlam below. He tilted his head slowly and peered heavenward as though he could sip some of the zesty sunlight and reap its benefits. It momentarily lifted his spirits, but he knew the tonic would not last. He had to plod on, scything and slashing his way forward, trampling the wet reeds and ferns, batting away the flies and peeling off the leeches. The brief respite from the shady gloom of the rainforest did nothing to alleviate his pain. His head throbbed with a dull, foggy ache; his lips and throat were parched; his right arm was racked with cramps from swinging the machete; his legs felt leaden and he could feel his feet rotting from days of walking in muddy mush. He knew he could not take much more and that at some point his body would give up, forcing him to collapse in a mouldering heap where he would join the undergrowth and fauna in the blissful joy of slumber. Whilst he still had strength, however, he would soldier on, smashing with his blade on a path that only seemed to lead deeper into the jungle.

For the first time on his journey he noticed that the ground beneath him began to slope downward whilst at the same time becoming wetter and more uneven. He could hear the sound of bubbling water. The shrubbery became less dense and gaps appeared that enabled him to push his way through without cutting. The ground became more level, but turned swamp-like, and he found himself up to his knees in a boggy brown soup. He waded on, drawn to the sight of darting black objects in the water. He was unable to tell if they were fish, rodents or snakes. A fetid smell that reeked of stagnation and decay attacked his senses, but he had no choice but to endure it.

The swamp eventually petered out and the terrain became firm again, opening up a clearing, the first of its kind since this nightmare began. It was surrounded by the same dark morass of growth, but it was an oasis of sorts. He sat on a boulder and enjoyed a brief interlude of badly-needed rest. He stared up at the sky, which had once again filled with menacing thunderclouds. As if to test his sanity, he spoke to himself, half expecting an answer.

"How did I get here? How did this begin?" he shouted deliriously, unable to recall anything about himself or the genesis of his journey. "Who put me here to witness this?" he yelled at the top of his voice. A brace of hummingbirds heard his cries and took fright, buzzing away into the sky. He got to his feet again and as he did so, noticed in the far corner of the clearing a myriad of fat black flies hovering over what appeared to be a decomposing lump of meat; an animal of some sort had died and the greedy midges were feasting on the carcass. Out of morbid curiosity, he approached the putrid hunk of flesh and gristle. Its shape appeared to resemble that of an ape or even a human. Because the skeleton was shattered and, in particular, the head was missing, it was hard to reach a definitive conclusion. The terrible stench made him recoil.

"How did this happen? Who was this?" he screamed, pointing helplessly at the disintegrating remains. "Who put me here?"

He resolved to plough on. He picked up his trusty machete and continued on his way. In order to break out of the forest wall that surrounded the clearing he had to pick a spot at random; only then could he start thrashing away again. He chose two spots that were so cluttered with gnarled roots and knotted branches that he simply could not advance any further. The third spot proved to be better and he was able to progress. After an hour or so of chopping and swearing, he found himself in another clearing, this one slightly larger than the last.

By this time the heavens had opened and he was showered in a warm tropical rain. The rain was so loud and intense that it managed to drown out the chirping and clicking of the omnipresent wildlife. Again, there were boulders that enabled him to take the weight off his feet, so he sat down, although the pause was hardly restful as the rain continued to batter him. He was about to get up when the rain abated abruptly. His eye was drawn to a puddle that had formed a few metres away in a small depression in the soil. He approached the water just as a few powerful rays of sunshine became visible from behind a dark cloud above, a rainbow appearing next to it. The light turned the puddle into a mirror and, without meaning to do so, he looked downward and caught a glimpse of himself and the rainbow, which reflected in the water. The fog that had befuddled his brain for so long suddenly lifted. He stared at his shabby uniform, battered cap and his jet-black oriental eyes and gasped. In a flash, he remembered who he was, what he was and what he had been doing before this nightmare began.

***

Lance Corporal John Watkins of the Royal Berkshire Regiment saluted as his superior approached him. The Burmese midday sun was beating down on them with considerable ferocity, but both maintained their military dignity. Over the course of the past year, both men had, to a degree, become acclimatised to the oppressive heat and humidity of the Far East, although their uniforms still seemed ill-suited for the environment. The Colonel's face was beetroot red and his steel-rimmed glasses shimmered in the sunlight.

"Well, what shall we do with the bugger, Watkins? He's a problem, isn't he?"

"Quite so, sir," replied Watkins, standing at attention. "We're not used to taking Jap prisoners. He wouldn't have surrendered if we hadn't caught him in this state." The men stared at the emaciated body of the comatose Japanese soldier lying in a wooden cage next to where they stood.

"Well, we can't take 'im with us. We don't 'ave the resources to cart him fifty miles up hill and down dale through the bloody jungle on a stretcher. We're under strict orders to move out of 'ere." The Colonel stroked his chin pensively. "The way 'e's been thrashing about in his cage for the past few days 'e's probably got malaria, but I'm certainly not wasting good quinine on the bastard. Sooner let 'im writhe in agony and let the soldier ants polish him off for lunch. I think we should just leave 'im, Watkins."

"But we can't leave him behind, sir. If we take him out of the cage, he might come round and make it back to his unit. I guess we could leave him in it to rot."

"You know, Watkins, we'd better deal with him now."

Watkins looked concerned. "But what about the Geneva Convention, sir?"

"I don't think he'll be too fussed about that, Watkins, and I'm certainly not," replied the Colonel as his right hand reached down into his holster for his Enfield Mark 1 revolver.

THE BEGINNING

Adam was in a bad mood. The walk to town was rarely pleasurable, and today was no exception. The road was especially dusty and tiny motes of sand and grit irritated his eyes and the undersides of his feet. In addition, one of his sandals rubbed against his toes, making the mere act of walking onerous. He needed new footwear but could not afford it. The early morning sun was already ferocious, he felt hot, bothered and generally uncomfortable even though the day had only just begun. Physical irritants aside, he had a strong sense of trepidation about his meeting later that morning because he knew needed to go well. If it did not, and he were to lose the confidence of those from whom he took orders, he would quickly find himself out of a job, impoverished or even worse. His beloved wife and his newborn child would not thank him if he could not deliver the bare essentials necessary for survival in what seemed to Adam to be an increasingly unforgiving world.

Adam's family dwelling was situated some distance from the town. The road to it was little more than a dirt track; it afforded no shade from the sun. Adam took a swig from his flagon of water, wiped his brow on his sleeve and tried to concentrate on preparing for the meeting. He had thought about it a lot the night before, and had even practiced how he would deliver his piece, but he well knew that these things never worked out the same in reality as they do in practice. Trudging along, he clung tightly to his bag, an item that comprised of little more than a rough piece of fabric scrunched up to enclose the contents within.

As the walls of the town came into sight, so did the lines of beggars on both sides of the road. They always congregated around the areas nearest the gates and they were in a truly pitiful state. Several were missing limbs. The females and males were indistinguishable by their makeshift clothing – their rags at were universally torn and filthy. They were emaciated, with blackened, toothless faces, matted hair and tearful eyes. As Adam marched through, along with a number of other well-to-do citizens, many beggars reached out with bowls, others with cupped hands, often with mutilated fingers. Some were too weak to make a begging gesture and instead stared at the passersby like ghosts, with their sunken cheeks, cracked lips and pleading facial gestures. One beggar, a young double amputee, rocked on his stumps and lunged towards Adam, causing him to stumble. Adam swiped him away firmly with his left hand and gave him a poignant scowl. Having been touched, Adam noted that the wretched man bore no tell-tale signs of leprosy, a serious concern whenever one came into contact with the lowest rungs of society.

Having negotiated his way past the scroungers and guttersnipes, Adam found himself at the gates to the town. The gates were well-manned by soldiers whose sole job it was to keep out those of a dubious nature, such as thieves, beggars, lepers, anyone of vaguely foreign appearance or anyone showing symptoms of illness. The soldiers were open to bribes, but generally did a good job distinguishing between respectable people going about their honest business and those who were not.

Once through the gates, Adam made his way along a cobblestone path into the heart of the town. Mercifully, the way was largely shaded although there were other aggravating factors to deal with, one being the all-pervading smell of sewerage, bodily odours and general waste. The town had become much more crowded in recent years, producing an increased volume of squalid litter, rubbish and other unhygienic by-products of human beings living in overcrowded conditions. There were also rats aplenty, although they preferred to make their sorties into the open during the cool of the evening. Other creatures such as cockroaches, mice, scorpions and flies were much less discriminating.

After passing through a number of haphazardly arranged winding streets, Adam came to the market square, a place that lifted his spirits. Although it was less busy today than other days, it was still crowded with stalls of all kinds selling everything under the sun, from exotic spices to melons, from fine necklaces to the meat of freshly slaughtered lambs. The merchants were always keen to promote their wares and the market was an invariably noisy place. That day was especially cacophonous because a fight had broken out. Adam quickly gathered that a thin fellow with a feisty appearance had been caught trying to steal a loaf of bread. The poor man was obviously impoverished and likely starving. He must have been desperate, for the likely penalty for his misdeed was death. Adam walked past the man, who was being dragged away by two soldiers. One held onto his arms while the other grabbed the man's long grey beard. The man hurled vile abuse at everyone around him and even managed to spit on Adam's lower garment, causing Adam to respond by kicking the thief in the ribs, an act of violence that he quickly regretted as a bolt of pain shot through his toes.

After leaving the market square, Adam eventually found himself in the cleaner, more salubrious part of town, where the atmosphere was more peaceful. There were neatly paved roads, carefully arranged olive trees, smart villas in place of shabby houses and well-dressed men and women, many displaying spoils of wealth such as fine clothes and jewellery. Adam did not often come here, but today was different. His appointment with an important political dignitary was unusually special. Adam had made a careful note of the location of the man's home and, having received the long-expected invitation to account for his activities, Adam wanted to leave nothing to chance and so he arrived in good time. The

Senator's residence was gated and guarded, but as soon as Adam gave his name to the guard he was saluted, greeted and welcomed into the villa. A young female slave with long, plaited black hair and a simple, yet attractive white dress escorted him to what appeared to be a waiting room. He was invited to sit on a beautifully crafted chair that was both padded and comfortable, a luxury Adam had never before experienced. He felt slightly awkward, as he was dirty from the journey and worried that his appearance and general state were out of place in such opulent surroundings. The white stone floors, the pond with fish and the walls covered with tapestries and paintings gave a firm impression to any visitor, including Adam, that the Senator was a man of immense riches. In Judea, riches equated to power, and Adam knew that he, by comparison, should feel honoured to be given the task bestowed upon him. He knew that this was more than luck. His great uncle, who had effected the initial introduction, was influential, albeit not excessively wealthy, and Adam had been carefully selected out of a number of other candidates. The mere fact that he was literate helped distinguish him, but it alone would not have been enough.

After being seated, a male slave gave Adam a chalice containing fresh water, which he drank with relish. The slave then offered to wash his feet, a service he politely declined. He was then given a bowl of grapes and dates that he decided to sample. He was not used to being treated like a king and resolved to make the most of the experience. Perhaps, if things went well and his lot improved, he might one day enjoy the finer things in life. He hardly dared to dream about such things.

After a long wait, Adam was ushered into a meeting room where he was once again invited to sit. He did so, but stood a few moments later as the Senator entered the room. He was a tall man with a shock of white hair, a stern face and boldly coloured garments. He spoke with a gruff, deep voice.

"Welcome, Adam. Thank you for coming. I hope your journey was not too tiresome?"

"No, not at all, sir," he replied.

"I hope you have been made comfortable. We'll have some more refreshments later."

"That sounds excellent, sir. Thank you."

"You are an intelligent fellow, Adam. I'll come to the point and then let you show me what you have done."

"Thank you, sir."

"I have trusted your judgment in this matter since I think you understand the problems we all face. I'm afraid that some of our contemporaries do not. Even some of my superiors prefer to ignore the realties all around us. You know my views. Our way of life is in peril. The fabric of our society is fragile. Natural resources, food and water are scarce. We face daily challenges from the elements, from diseases, from failed harvests, from foreigners who would gladly plunder these lands and from those within who wish to do the same. We are all at risk but, as you well know Adam, the most immediate problem is the rabble, the great unwashed, whose lives are plagued by the worst effects of poverty. They will unseat us given half the chance. The soothsayers tell me that the warning signs are written in the stars. The gods are displeased with us. There is trouble in the air, and we need to quell the revolution before it happens. We need a solution to this problem. We need fresh ideas."

"Indeed, sir. This is what you explained to me when we last met, and I believe I understand the issue. You rightly believe that brute force only goes so far."

Adam could feel his heart beating heavily in his chest as he spoke, and he knew that the moment was about to come he would be required to expound upon his theory. He had no idea what the reaction was likely to be.

"Sir, you asked me to think of a novel way to subdue the rabble. I have the germ of an idea, but it needs developing. The way I see it, there is a general dearth of food, clothing and shelter. Those are the harsh facts of life that we cannot easily remedy. In my view, there is only one other form of sustenance that we can supply to the masses to appease them, and that is spiritual sustenance."

The Senator raised an eyebrow but appeared interested. Adam continued. "I have prepared something to show you. There is more work to be done – much more hard work – but this is a start, and I will continue if you like the idea." Adam then proceeded to unfurl the package he had brought with him and seconds later unrolled the pieces of parchment that lay within. He opened the first sheet and proceeded to read aloud:

"In the beginning God created the heavens and the earth and the earth was without form and void and darkness was upon the face of the deep, and the Spirit of God moved upon the face of the waters. Then God said: 'Let there be light'; and there was light."

A Demand with Menaces

James lay on a battered old mattress on the cold stone floor in a corner of the room. He had adopted a rather dramatic foetal position. He was still wearing his navy blue work suit, white shirt and maroon tie, though his suit was horribly dishevelled and crumpled. His shirt was hanging out and his tie was grubby and frayed. His face was covered in dirty stubble; his hair was a greasy mess and one of his eyes was blackened. The atmosphere was dank and although the walls comprised of white tiles, they were stained with yellow streaks, giving them something of a urinal quality. The solitary window was high, out of reach and covered in dust. Insipid, greenish daylight seeped through the aperture but it did little to illuminate the room. A dim electric bulb in the ceiling provided some additional light but not enough to lift the all-pervading sense of dinginess.

Paul stared at James and lit his third stinking French cigarette in a row whilst pondering how best to take a suitable photograph of James. He took a reading from the light meter on his camera and then considered different angles in order to assess which one would work best. He swore each time he moved position, eventually opting for a spot in the middle of the room where he locked the camera in place on a tripod. James' body was suddenly bathed in a burst of bluish white light as Paul pressed the flash button. The whole process looked almost professional. Paul took several more photographs, intending to capture the spotlight on the front page of The Times newspaper. Paul fiddled with his camera bag, took a couple more pictures for good luck and started packing away his equipment.

"I'll be back in a few minutes," said Paul, screwing the dust cover onto one of the lenses. James said nothing.

Paul retreated to a nearby room that was equally squalid and badly lit, where he joined his partner in crime, David, who was seated at a cheap wooden desk playing with bits of paper and glue.

"A couple of these beauties should do the trick," Paul said to David, showing him a quick slide show of the pictures on the screen at the back of the camera.

"Yep, they look good," replied David. "Print a few of them off and let's see what they look like. I've got a good feeling about this. As you can see, my note is nearly finished. I like the old fashioned blackmail format, don't you? I could have knocked out something on the computer but it wouldn't have had the same effect, would it?"

David showed Paul the A4 sheet he had been working on, and he saw that each letter of the note was cut from a magazine and pasted onto the paper. The note was unambiguous:

We are holding your husband, Mrs. Anderson.

We will kill him if you contact the police. We will supply you with instructions for payment soon. We will kill him if you fail to follow those instructions.

Do not do anything stupid.

David then folded the note and put it into a plain white envelope.

***

It was Saturday. Julia Anderson sat white-faced and distraught on the leather sofa in the plush living room of the detached house she shared with her husband in Weybridge, Surrey. She was nursing a stiff gin and tonic, even though it was not yet lunchtime. James had been missing for two days and the police, it seemed to her, had done little more than pay lip service to the notion of finding her beloved spouse. She had explained at length that it was completely out of character for her husband to not call; he would always do so, even if he was only going to be held up at work for an hour or so. The fact that he had vanished into thin air meant that something awful must have occurred.

More than an hour after a bundle of post landed on the floor of her hall Julia picked up and nearly disregarded what looked appeared to be a thick wad of junk mail. For some reason, however, her eye was caught by a white envelope amongst the other items. She opened it and read the note with a mixture of disbelief and horror. She struggled to overcome her natural sense of shock, but managed to telephone the police and explain herself clearly without breaking into tears. They will finally sit up and take notice, she thought to herself. Indeed, within twenty minutes someone identified as Detective Inspector Farrand was standing in her doorway alongside a young female police constable.

"Good morning, Mrs. Anderson," said the Detective Inspector, after introducing himself and his colleague.

"Please, come this way," Julia replied, leading the pair through to her living room.

"Can I offer anyone a drink?" she asked, slightly embarrassed by her half-empty tumbler.

"Don't trouble yourself, Mrs. Anderson," said the Detective Inspector in a soothing voice. "Just explain to us what's happened."

"There's very little to say, Inspector. As you know, I reported my husband missing two days ago and have hardly slept a wink since. I had no idea what might have happened until this note arrived." Julia handed over the blackmail note and gave the two police officers a moment to read it.

The Detective Inspector pursed his lips, re-read the note and paused before speaking.

"Mrs. Anderson, I'm afraid to say that these sorts of incidents are not as uncommon as you might imagine. Very few attract publicity because no one involved ever has any interest in speaking about them. The perpetrators are invariably concerned with one thing and one thing only: money. With careful handling, we'll get your husband back safely but it will take time and you will need to be patient. It's rare for a kidnap victim in these cases to be harmed. He's the prized asset, and the kidnappers know it. Tell us a little about your husband, Mrs. Anderson. Whoever these people are, they have been planning this crime for some time and they may have slipped up and made a mistake somewhere in the process. They often do. Tell us a little bit about the background to your husband's business."

"Well, Inspector. I'm not sure how much I can tell you. My husband's a successful, self-made businessman. He set up an insurance brokerage back in the 1990s after learning the tricks of the trade from working at a big company in his youth. His firm went from strength to strength over the years and he has never looked back. I don't think he has any enemies but we are not hard up, Inspector, so I guess that makes him an easy target for blackmail."

"I'm afraid it does. The kidnappers will have thought about this very carefully. They must have identified a pot of gold. I use the plural when referring to your husband's kidnappers because it's highly unlikely that this sort of operation would be carried out by an individual. It generally requires a team effort. Another question, if I may: do you know much about your husband's business activity on a day-to-day basis? His whereabouts at any given time, for example?"

"Not really. He tells me what he's up to, but I don't keep tabs on him if that's what you mean, Inspector."

"Hm. Give us some thinking time, Mrs. Anderson, but let me tell you what'll happen next. You'll soon receive a demand for money. Probably for several million pounds, I would imagine. I'm sorry to be crude about the subject but, if it were necessary to produce large sums of cash, even as bait, would you be able to do that, Mrs. Anderson?"

"No, I would not, Inspector. We have some wealth, but very few liquid assets. Indeed, over the past few months even James has been moaning about supposed cash flow problems. In short, we are not awash with cash. Not that kind of money."

"And what about kidnap insurance, Mrs. Anderson? Is there any chance that your husband might have arranged for coverage? If so, you'll need to notify them immediately," said the young constable, piping up for the first time.

"What I do know is that James is very good about protecting us with the right kind of insurance, so I believe we have a policy to cover this sort of thing. Given the nature of his business, I guess you'd rather expect that of him, wouldn't you?"

"Indeed," said the Detective Inspector, stroking his chin in contemplation.

***

David strapped James' hand into position using the arm of a chair and the tightest notch of a leather belt. Paul fetched the fireman's axe, a vicious instrument with a bright red handle and black head. James was conscious, but with nearly three quarters of a bottle of Johnny Walker in his bloodstream, he was dribbling and his head lolled around. His eyes were glazed over, but it was clear from the grimace on his face that he knew what was about to happen.

"For the life of me, I cannot believe that the freaking insurance company is not taking this seriously," said David. "We've been reasonable, very reasonable, but they obviously think we're a bunch of jokers."

"They're all the same. They love to take our premiums but when it comes to paying out on a claim they suddenly become stingy Scrooges. Bastards!" remarked Paul in response.

James closed his eyes and tightly clenched his right fist, bracing himself for the blow. David held James' right arm and positioned the little finger towards the edge of the wooden chopping block. A split second later, Paul slammed down the axe and, with a sickening click, James' severed finger dropped to the floor. James ruddy face suddenly blanched and, after a moment of delayed reaction, he squealed with pain as David quickly administered a bandage to the remaining stump.

"You'll be fine," said David to James. He offered James another swig, but he instead pushed the bottle away with an angry shove.

Paul coolly picked up the finger from the floor and carefully placed it in a small, transparent plastic bag.

"If this doesn't convince them nothing will," exclaimed Paul, holding the bag and its contents up to the light.

"I bloody hope so," said David.

"Me too," said James with surprising clarity. "The things we do for money."

CHRISTMAS

"Christmas wouldn't be Christmas without any presents," said Amir. "I know it's not my religion, but I love Christmas presents and, in a peculiar sort of way I suppose I love the whole ridiculous Christmas thing – the Great Escape and all. I guess that having been brought up in a country that worships everything from Christmas trees to cards depicting snowy Dickensian scenes, it's hardly surprising that I've got a soft spot for Yuletide paraphernalia. I know that sounds weird. Could you pass the scissors?"

"Well, it is my religion, and I love everything to do with Christmas, too," said Christine. "For me it's all about the food. I have a terrible weakness for mince pies. I especially love the ones made with puff pastry, stuffed with deep filling and sprinkled with icing sugar. Give me one of those with a strong cup of tea and I'm in heaven. My other obsession is with Christmas pudding, which I think is divine - the richer the better - and a blob of thick cream never goes amiss with it. So, who are you wrapping this present for?"

"Oh, it's for my uncle. He's a lonely old soul. He absolutely loves cooking, so I bought him a food processor. It's far too late to send it to him by post so I thought I'd deliver it to him personally. He lives in Central London, so it's only a tube ride away. I thought it'd be a nice surprise for him."

"Well, I have to say that's very thoughtful of you. I'm quite sure your uncle will appreciate the kind gesture."

Amir picked up a large roll of Christmas wrapping paper. It was shiny, bright red and covered in white snowflakes of various shapes and sizes. He meticulously cut off a suitable length of paper and then, with the neatness and precision of someone who does gift wrapping for a job, Amir proceeded to lay it on the dining room table before placing the large box on top of it. He made a number of judicious cuts and folds and the end product looked beautiful. He sealed it with two invisible strips of sticky tape at either end and gave it an attractive finishing touch using glossy silver ribbon and a small handmade rosette on top.

"There," announced Amir smiling with pride. "That looks just about perfect, even though I say so myself. If you're going to do a job, do it properly." Amir looked outside. He saw a few flurries of sleet swirling around in the breeze. "Typical London weather at Christmas: wet sleet that will inevitably be followed by slush. It's such a pity that we so rarely get proper snow in London, although I suppose the entire transport system would grind to a halt if we did."

He looked at his watch. "Look, I had better be on my way. Feel free to make yourself at home here if you like. I think I saw that White Christmas will be on the telly a bit later. It doesn't get much more Christmassy than that. It's on BBC2, I believe. You can't miss that if you're a real Christmas traditionalist. Also there are some mince pies in the kitchen cupboard if you fancy one. I'll be back in a couple of hours." Christine's instant response was a look of disappointment.

"Oh, you can't go on your own Amir. I'll keep you company if you like. It'll be so boring going into town without company. In fact, it'll be particularly unpleasant since you'll hit the rush hour if you leave now."

"Oh, don't worry, Christine. You don't need to come with me. My uncle's a miserable old sod. It won't be a very exciting outing."

"I'll tell you what. I've got the DVD of White Christmas. I'll come with you to town and then we can go back to my place and watch it afterwards. I'll make some dinner, put a log on the fire and Bob's your uncle, so to speak."

"If you really insist, but you simply don't have to. I'd actually rather you didn't."

"You are a funny fish, Amir. Don't be a loner. It'll be fine. Here, grab your jacket and woolly hat and let's go."

Amir and Christine donned their outdoor clothes, inclusive of scarves and gloves. Amir took another look at his watch and reached for the present, wincing slightly as he lifted it. They left Amir's flat and headed left towards Wood Green tube station via the High Street that was heaving with Christmas shoppers. It was getting dark now and the falling sleet was intensifying. Christine looked up at the multi-coloured street lights that shimmered on high, draped across the road.

"They've actually done a rather wonderful job this year, don't you think? Rather striking, and not too tacky in my opinion. I love the dancing reindeer."

"Do you think that Jesus would have approved?"

"You know, Amir, sometimes you are so predictable. I could rise to the bait but I'm just not in the mood. I'm enjoying this Winter Wonderland in my own simplistic way and I'm not going to let you spoil it with a stupid discussion about religion. Talk about something else."

"I also enjoy the festive spirit, but I struggle with all this hysterical Western materialism. It's got no soul. I'm sorry, Christine. I'm really sorry."

"You don't have anything to apologise for. You are behaving strangely. You know what? Instead of watching White Christmas perhaps we should watch It's a Wonderful Life with James Stewart. It's got a bit of depth. You'll really enjoy it. I'm sure you will"

"I've obviously heard of it, but it's just one of those films I've never got around to watching. What's it actually about?"

"Oh, it's about a very depressed man who's about to kill himself just before Christmas. He's visited by an angel who saves him after demonstrating that the world would be a poorer place without him. It's corny, but brilliant. You'll really enjoy it, I promise you will."

Amir said nothing.

They eventually made it to the entrance of the tube station. A bearded old man with ginger hair and a filthy brown duffel coat had parked himself on the pavement just outside. He wore a piece of rope for a belt and somewhat incongruous open sandals. He also had a battered hat that he placed next to a cardboard sign on which he'd written the words "Hungry and Homeless" in thick, black felt pen. Christine had nearly walked past the man, but halted when Amir stopped.

"Could you hold this a second?" asked Amir, handing the present to Christine. "I need to get my wallet out. I'll only be a second"

"This is bloody heavy," she replied as she received the present with both hands. Amir reached into a pocket inside his coat and pulled out his wallet. To Christine's astonishment, he emptied the entire contents of the wallet into the bearded man's hat, including several twenty-pound notes and a pile of silver change.

"Thank you, gov'. Thank you very much. God bless you," said the man with obvious gratitude.

"You sure are feeling generous today!" commented Christine. "Perhaps the spirit of Christmas has got to you after all."

There was more seasonal activity inside the station, where a group of young school children were singing *God Rest Ye Merry Gentlemen* in dulcet tones, led by a man dressed as Santa. Christine threw a handful of coins into the collection bucket.

She and Amir then weaved their way through the crowd, past the ticket barrier, then down the escalator. They travelled on the Piccadilly Line, standing on a packed train and then they changed onto the Victoria Line at Finsbury Park. The journey was uneventful, save for the unwanted entertainment of two drunken youths singing obscene songs at the top of their voices.

At Finsbury Park they boarded an equally unpleasant and overcrowded carriage where again they had to stand. Christine found herself awkwardly pressed against Amir with the present crushed between them. The atmosphere was extremely stuffy. Whilst she tried to distract herself with happy thoughts about the Christmas shopping she still had to do, Amir mumbled to himself and looked distracted.

The train trundled along slowly in a stop-start fashion until it finally ground to a halt just before Oxford Circus. The driver announced on the intercom system that they were being held at a red signal for a couple of minutes due to a defective train ahead. The engines stopped and, for once, the carriage became quiet. It was then that Christine heard a muffled rhythmic sound nearby. She took a moment to try and place the sound. She looked at Amir's face and noticed the beads of sweat on his forehead. He was grimacing, as if he were in acute pain. She looked him in the eye and spoke her words purposefully:

"Amir. You said this thing for your uncle is a food processor. Why is it ticking?"

THE SWIMMER

He was shivering like crazy in the wild, freezing cold water although the very act of swimming was, to some extent at least, keeping him warmer than would otherwise have been the case. He tried to ensure that his arm and leg movements were not just energetic and animated – they were ferocious. He pounded the waves as hard as he could in an attempt to generate some kind of heat, anything to relieve the icy pain that was chilling him to the bone. The suppressed but logical segments of his brain told him that he could not keep going for too much longer. Not that he could stop now. Stopping was not an option because stopping meant dying and he was not yet ready to die.

The most frustrating thing was that the choppy turbulence of the water made it almost impossible to snatch a glimpse of the mainland for anything more than a fleeting second or two. When he did manage to catch sight of it, the outline was shrouded in a murky mist but that was just about enough to raise his spirits. The mass of land to which he was aiming seemed to be getting nearer or was he just imaging that? The dawn sky, a pale grey canvass, was smudged with a fuzzy blob of ochre low on the horizon. If he was sure of anything it was that if he steered his aching body towards the sun, he would reach the land. Deranged thoughts had crept into his head telling him that once ashore, the sun would bathe him in glorious warmth and he would bask in its radiance and he would be restored.

Having gulped far too much dirty salt water he decided that he would swim on his back for a few minutes. The waves had calmed down a little and, adopting a new position would give him a rest of sorts, or at least a little respite from his more furious exertions. He twisted his body around and, still applying a degree of power to overcome the strength of the currents that swirled beneath him, he moved himself onto his back. The life force of the briny water was determined to drag him out into the bay and from there out to sea where he would perish and become fish food. He quickly realised that his backstroke was not strong enough and that however much he attempted to head towards the general direction of the sun, the mighty pull of the tide would take him inexorably the wrong way, out into the greenish brown wilderness. He cursed and spat bile but turned over again and as he did so he spied a small motor boat at a distance of about three hundred yards or so, wending its way from the mainland to the rock. It was close enough for him to make out the detail of two people on board the deck of the vessel. One looked like a woman with a flowing green scarf that flapped violently in the wind. The other appeared to be an official of some kind with a peaked cap and a grey tunic. The woman was pointing out to sea. He toyed with the idea of lowering his profile or even diving under the water but then he surmised that the chances of anyone on the boat noticing him in the water were virtually zero. They wouldn't even think to look in the water because being in the water was madness beyond the contemplation of normal decent people. He was in the water because he was not like them and never had been. In fact he had been in deep water up to his neck, swimming against the tide, for most of his life; it was just that this particular tide was very physical and very tangible and it was out to kill him if he gave it half a chance. He pushed on against the water, ploughing his way through the swell, sweeping the muddy torrents behind him.

In an effort to keep himself going he attempted to cast his mind back to his early high school days when he had swum for the school in a number of competitive races, some even against other schools. They allowed him that privilege. He had disgraced himself at every subject that any teacher tried to teach him but swimming was his strong suit – a redeeming skill for which he was always praised despite his other failings. He had been brought up as a swimmer by his father – a brutal but fit man who had taught him the breaststroke and later the crawl, at a very early age. He had quickly become a fearless swimmer – jumping off rocks into lakes, swimming in dangerous rivers, diving into water anywhere – especially places where there were signs saying "No Diving". He recalled one particular occasion when he was about ten years old; he had been showing off to his friends and he had dived recklessly into a stream only to crack his forehead on an invisible underwater rock. The head wound knocked him out but he regained consciousness only to find himself choking on water and struggling to stay afloat. His friend Eddie had quickly clambered down and pulled him from the water, dragging him by his arms onto the grassy bank of the river and unceremoniously dumping him there like a half-drowned rat. No one other than the Grim Reaper was going to rescue him from his current predicament. There was no Eddie or anyone like him. He was alone in this battle of endurance and he was either going to make it to the shore and win, or die in the attempt. In an odd way there was something rather satisfyingly simple in the notion that there was no halfway house.

Having made an extra effort to overcome an especially strong current he reached a point in the crossing at which the currents subsided a little and he decided to tread water for a minute or so simply to recharge his batteries. He needed to take stock and could just about do so because the waves had momentarily become smaller than they had been less than a minute ago. The waters were temperamental and capricious so he could not tarry for too long but he needed to assess his prospects if only to inspire himself. He wanted to believe that there was a chance, however remote, that he might survive his ordeal and achieve the unthinkable. No one else had. He could see on the one hand the distinct shape of the island and the ghastly man-made structure that blighted it and on the other, the increasingly clear view of the shore that was now appreciably closer. He was way beyond halfway now, the point of no return – not that returning was ever an option. He tried to resolve that even if it was the last thing he ever did, he would make it to the shore even if he dropped dead there and then from exhaustion or hypothermia. He was going to survive long enough to touch *terra firma* again. He wasn't quite ready to go to heaven, or more likely hell of course.

Just as his hopes were raised they were dashed in an instant. The transitory lull was suddenly replaced by fresh gusts of inbound sea air that whipped up the water into a stormy and unsettled brew and left him clawing and scrambling helplessly in the foamy rolling waves. He was defenceless against the buffeting and he was left with no choice but to swim harder, battling on as best he could. He knew that he was Canute-like in his impotence, trying to defy the laws of physics, odds that were plainly stacked against him, odds that seemed determined to condemn him to death by drowning. The wind whistled through him as though he were porous, stabbing him with icy daggers, punishing him for trying to behave with such impertinence, flouting the power of the elements, spurning the natural order of things even though he was nothing more than a lowly mortal. At the mercy of the waves and the unpredictable whims of the tempestuous currents he knew that he would probably soon be broken. A vicious wave tossed him over and he went plunging head first into the deep but, a minute or so later, his lungs searing with pain, he bobbed up again, gasping for air, his muscles weakened, his ears throbbing, his vision blurred. He found himself much closer to the shore than he had dared to imagine was possible only a few minutes earlier – by a stroke of good fortune the water had swept him inland and it was continuing to do so and the sight of the mainland ahead gave him an adrenalin rush that he was now sure would power him on to safety, now only a few hundred yards away. He was already starting to think of a plan as to what to do once he had made it to dry land. His trump card was that no one could possibly conceive of the idea that he had swum the treacherous mile and a half across the bay and that perceived impossibility would make his disappearance from the face of the Earth all the more feasible. He was about to become a member of one of the most select clubs on the planet – an escapee from Alcatraz, missing, presumed dead.

BACK TO SCHOOL

It was one of those beautifully crisp autumnal mornings. The sky was a deep shade of electric blue and a pale yellow sun, partially eclipsed by thin sheaths of cirrus clouds, beamed down on a corner of North London that was buzzing with noise, traffic, commuters, children, shoppers and mothers with pushchairs. Howard Stapleton sat alone at the back on the top deck of the bus gathering his thoughts. He shared the vehicle with at least thirty garrulous schoolchildren and a handful of senior citizens. He had been staring out of the window for much of the journey, wondering what the day ahead would hold. He was anxious. Although he had attempted to dress reasonably smartly, Howard felt self-conscious about his ill-fitting suit, his rather unfashionable raincoat and his brown brogues, the left one of which was pinching on his big toe. His leather holdall was not just heavy but cumbersome.

The bus finally came to a halt at the bus stop where Howard had to get off. Along with all of the children who had also been on board, Howard stepped off the bus at the junction of Medway Road and Middleton Way, fifty yards or so from the entrance to Oakhouse Comprehensive School.

At a distance the school looked exactly the same as it always had – red brick, built in the 1930s, utilitarian and functional. He'd driven past it a few times in recent years but without going in of course.

Howard's heart fluttered as he reached the school gates having last walked through them when he left school at the end of his sixth form on 7th July 1978. He vividly remembered wiping a few tears from his eyes as he had done so. He had enjoyed school and recalled being hugely fearful of what lay ahead – it was so obviously the end of an era.

Although some of the window frames had changed and the guttering had been freshly painted, even at close quarters there were no obvious alterations to the school that had etched itself in his memory three decades earlier.

Near the entrance a small boy, perhaps aged twelve or so, was doing up his shoelaces as Howard approached. His foot was perched on a step. His uniform looked new and clean. His trousers had a visibly sharp crease.

"Hello," said Howard. "Who are you?" The boy peered at him with deep suspicion and with a look on his face that made it quite clear that he did not recognise Howard.

"My name is Williamson, Sir. Marc Williamson."

"And what class are you in Williamson?"

"I'm in Form 2c, Sir. Mr. Baker is my new form teacher."

"I see. Mr. Baker eh," responded Howard, bluffing his way along. "Well Williamson. I'd like you to show me the way to the Headmaster's office. I was a pupil here a long time ago but I'm not sure I can remember where it is. I'd be very grateful if you would be my guide."

"Of course, Sir," answered the boy unquestioningly. "Can I help with your bag?" he asked, assuming Howard to be someone of importance.

"No, don't worry but thank you anyway. I'll manage."

As they entered the school, they found themselves in a rather gloomy passageway with classrooms off to the right along an adjacent corridor. Out of the window, to the left, Howard spied several rows of metal cycle racks, many of them occupied by children's cycles of different colours and types. He distinctly recalled that thirty-one years ago the space had been taken up by a wooden bike shed and the crumbling remains of a World War Two air raid shelter. But it wasn't the bikes as such that triggered his memories. It was that precise location. To the left of the sheds was a quiet alcove that had not changed at all. This was the unforgettable place where Howard had experienced his first proper kiss. He remembered the incident as though it had happened yesterday. As part of a playground game of dare, Howard, then aged eleven, had found himself cornered by Jacqueline Squires, the object of his very first crush. Fortuitously for him, it was clear that the attraction appeared to be mutual but as to what was supposed to happen next, Howard was clueless. When the crucial moment came, Howard was simply unable to move any part of his body, least of all his lips, and found himself frozen by an unfamiliar cocktail of fear and excitement. Unfazed by Howard's paralysis, Jacqueline Squires had carried on regardless, planting her lips on his for a full five seconds. Howard's abiding memory was of closing his eyes during the process and opening them again a few seconds later only to discover that the delectable Jacqueline had vanished into thin air, as if by magic.

"This way, Sir," said the boy, snapping Howard out of his daydream and leading him past a quadrangle outside to the right. There was a patch of grass, some benches and a drinking fountain but nothing else.

"What happened to the tuck shop?" asked Howard. "There used to be a tuck shop out there that was opened up during playtime and manned by the school caretaker. Every day I used to buy a packet of cheese and onion crisps and, in the summer, a cherry-flavoured Jubbly."

"A Jubbly, Sir?" asked the boy, clearly perplexed. "What's a Jubbly?"

"It was a sort of big ice lolly in a cardboard container that was, well, kind of triangular shaped."

"I see," said the boy, now starting to doubt not only the credentials of the man he was escorting but also the man's sanity. Was he perhaps a fantasist of some sort? "There's no tuck shop here. Never has been as far as I know."

The odd pair continued along another corridor towards an open communal area. The boy was about to lead Howard straight through it when Howard suddenly stopped dead in his tracks.

"Crikey," he exclaimed. "I've just had another remarkable flashback. He doubled back on himself, closely followed by the boy who was starting to wonder if he shouldn't report the strange man to a member of staff without further ado. Howard paused for a second then scanned the scene around him. His line of vision alighted on a window on the far side of the room in an obscure corner that twisted round towards a flight of stairs. Howard went up to the window and started feeling with his hands on the underside of the windowsill. The boy stared at him incredulously.

"Can I help you, Sir? What are you looking for exactly?"

"Well Williamson," said Howard. "It's like this you see. On my very last day at Oakhouse I wedged a big piece of pink bubble gum under this window sill. I always wondered if it would still be here many years later. Well here I am and...yes, remarkably, it is still here after all these years. No reason why it shouldn't be I suppose eh Williamson?" The boy's expression of bewilderment was completely lost on Howard who was now starting to rather enjoy his nostalgic journey back in time.

"Perhaps we should get a move on, Sir?" said the boy, looking at his watch and pulling a face that indicated concern at the prospect of being late.

"Of course," said Howard. "Lead the way. We wouldn't want you to be late for Mr. Baker."

The next corridor led past the Great Hall where Howard once again had to pause as the memories came flooding back. The grandiose oak-panelled space was where assemblies were held. There was room for approximately one thousand students at the ground level and at least another three hundred on the balcony above. One end was adorned by a huge organ and a space where the choir sat. At the other end was the stage, the back of which was hidden from view by a vast mauve velvet curtain. Howard stepped inside to get a better look but the boy hung back knowing that the Great Hall was out of bounds before assembly.

"This is where I sat my exams in the summer of '76. They were called O-levels in those days - the equivalent of GCSEs today. The heat wave of '76. It was so hot that they had to open up every door and window just to get some oxygen in. I remember the teachers coming round with ice cold water and one girl fainting. What happy days!"

"How interesting," said the boy with barely concealed indifference. "If we could move on now Sir I would be grateful. My classroom is back at the other end of the school and morning registration is in about two minutes. I would hate to upset my new form teacher."

"Indeed," replied Howard. "You really must forgive me. Do carry on. I'm with you."

The boy led Howard to a quieter area, a short walk away from the Great Hall. The boy quickened his pace and Howard followed, the two of them attracting a quick glance from a couple of pupils and two teachers.

"Well here we are," said the boy, pointing to a room off to the right, the door of which was slightly ajar. It was clear that the office was empty. "There's no one here at the moment I'm afraid," said the boy after looking both ways. A new Headmaster starts today and I'm afraid I've forgotten his name. We were told. I'm sure he'll be along shortly if you'd like to wait here."

"I'm sure he will," replied Howard beaming broadly.

THE END

Lucy opened her eyes in a flash having suddenly been snapped out of a very deep slumber. Something extremely unusual had woken her up. There had been a deep rumbling vibration from within the ground that had, quite literally, shaken her out of her sleep. The sensation troubled her profoundly. She had an excellent scent for potential danger and had no hesitation in deciding that whatever the cause of the disturbance, it was not good. She could sense it in her bones. She could feel it. She could smell it. Indeed the smell was physical; the air was tainted by a nasty acrid odour that Lucy struggled to place. She didn't like it.

The strange vibrations started to diminish in strength as soon as Lucy was fully awake and alert. They then gradually faded away and finally stopped completely.

Lucy's eyes felt gritty but not in the way that they often did when she woke up. This was different. She blinked several times and the irritation diminished. She then began to survey the scene that surrounded her.

The red wall-to-wall carpet in the room was covered in millions of fragments of broken glass. Some of the tiny pieces caught the daylight and sparkled. There were also large slivers of glass scattered across the floor, strewn around the room like crystal daggers.

The windows to the room had shattered inwards leaving jagged remains in the window frames. As a result, cool air was wafting in from outside. The curtains were in tatters and the stripped remains flapped about making a rustling sound as they did so. Lucy could see that the sky outside was dark grey and filled with huge billowing black clouds. She moved slowly and cautiously in the direction of the broken windows trying to avoid the larger shards of glass that blocked the way. She peered out. The lawn in the garden was covered in greyish white flakes of a kind that that Lucy did not recognise. There was no sign of anything moving. Lucy retreated gingerly back into the room, unsure which way to turn.

Lucy then turned her gaze upwards towards the ceiling and noticed that a large crack had appeared there. It zig-zagged its way across the room in a broken diagonal line. The curious pattern stretched from one corner of the living room ceiling to the area just above the door on the other side. Small fragments of plaster and minute particles of dust floated down from above. Lucy could see that at one point along the crack, a beam of wood had become exposed as result of the fracture.

The walls were not damaged in the same way as the ceiling although the one adjacent to the windows did not look quite right. It was as though it were no longer perpendicular to the floor. A large picture depicting something blue and abstract had slumped down to one side although the frame still clung to the wall by a wire at the back that was visibly still hooked over a nail. The heavy door to the room that had been shut was now ajar but it was wedged open at an oblique angle, as though it had been whacked by some colossal force.

Lucy could also detect a troubling creaking sound from somewhere within the house. She was unsure whether she should venture out of the room or simply wait for someone to come to her. She initially decided on a passive course and stood still. The evil smell that had struck her nostrils as soon as she woke up was becoming noticeably more pungent – it was obviously drifting in through the broken windows. It made the prospect of going outside unappealing. She remained still for a few minutes, completely bewildered and disorientated by the chaos around her. She tried to make sense of the mess. What on Earth is going on?

The creaking sound beyond the door suddenly became louder and was followed by a deafening crash. Lucy cowered in the corner farthest away from the door, quivering at the prospect of what strange occurrence might next take place. She had never been so frightened. Eventually her survival instinct prevailed and she decided that staying put in the room was not an option. Lucy knew she had to get away from the enclosed space of the room and see what was happening beyond its confines.

She reluctantly got to her feet and crept towards the narrow space left open by the door. She tried to nudge the door open but it was jammed in position. The gap was just wide enough for her to squeeze through.

The scene that she encountered in the hall was one of complete mayhem and destruction. The walls were blackened, as though scorched by an almighty flame. Part of the ceiling had collapsed and clear daylight was visible through the broken hole that looked as though it had been punched in by a blow from above. There were no windows at all, only more shattered glass strewn across the wooden floor along with broken rafters, masonry, pieces of plaster and other black and brown debris of varying shapes. One of Lucy's feet touched an oddly shaped piece of rubble and she flinched realising in an instant that it was boiling hot. She peered upwards to what remained of the stairs but there was little more than a chaotic pile of timber and carpet into which the iron banisters had fallen. The large chandelier that had once lit up the hall had collapsed and on top of its remains were piled lumps of concrete and a thick layer of dust. The dust was everywhere and Lucy had to squint in order to avoid getting too much in her eyes. There was no one in sight and it was very plain to Lucy that she urgently needed to get out of the house – away from the charred bedlam and into the open air.

The front door appeared to still be intact although it looked a darker shade of brown than normal. Lucy pushed against it with her body and, without hardly any use of force, the heavy slab of wood crashed outwards leaving a clear escape route into the front garden.

The front lawn, like the one at the rear, was decked in a greyish white substance, as was everything else in sight. Other things had changed. The huge tree that once adorned the far corner had been reduced to a blackened skeleton of twisted branches. The trunk was split and piles of what had once been its leaves, were heaped underneath it. The wooden fence that had surrounded the garden had disappeared completely and the scene beyond the garden was unclear as it seemed to be shrouded in fog. Lucy could feel her heart pounding. She was completely at sea, unsure whether to return to the ruined house or venture on into the mist. She stopped and looked around her but found no inspiration. She stared up again at the angry sky that was still awash with huge swirling black clouds. The sun, low on the horizon, was trying to pierce through the gloom but was blocked out by a pall of what looked like mushroom-coloured smoke. Lucy knew that the path past the ruined tree led down to the park and she opted to take her chances by leaving the relative safety of the territory that was well known to her. Although she had been distracted by the catastrophic changes, Lucy's mind was now starting to think about food and water. Perhaps she would find something in the park. She opted to go quickly even though the way ahead was misty.

After turning a corner she came to a patch where the fog had cleared and she heard the muffled but unmistakable sound of barking. Her head darted in every direction and soon she realised that although the noise was unclear, it was in fact nearby. Moving on Lucy encountered five growling dogs that were huddled around something lying on the floor. Ignoring the danger she approached the scene only to discover that the thing lying on the ground was a human and the five hungry hounds were eating it. Worse than that, even though half its face had been devoured and its clothes were ripped apart, Lucy could immediately tell that the human was her Master.

ALBERT

It was very early in the morning but Albert could see through the crack in the curtains that it was still pitch black outside. He stood wearing nothing but his underwear, his unsightly paunch spilling over at the front. He arched his back in a stretching motion and then flexed his hands, clicking his fingers as he did so. After a few moments of quiet contemplation he moved towards to the sink in the corner of the room. He hated staying in crummy hotels in London but the budget of three shillings and sixpence allocated to him by the Department did not permit anything more salubrious. For one night he could put up with it. Not that his home in Manchester was anything special.

Through the faint mist created by the steam from the soapy hot water in his sink, Albert stared at himself in the mirror for several seconds. For no particular reason he had become prone to examining his face first thing in the morning, as if by doing so he would gain some insight into his true character. He looked into his eyes, imagining perhaps that he could detect signs of some hidden emotion: sadness, joy, regret, disappointment, hope or guilt. In fact, despite peering as hard as he could, he could see no traces of any such sentiments. Not that he expected to do so. On the contrary, to his mind, his grey pupils seemed to have acquired a somewhat pale dullness in recent years and, if anything, they displayed nothing but ordinariness.

Using a broken piece of carbolic soap and a rough flannel he then proceeded to wash and wipe his face and then the rest of his torso. He scrubbed his fingernails with a nailbrush. Albert knew very well that he was a creature of habit who always carried in his bag of toiletries the essentials which included a nailbrush, hand-cream, a nail file, brilliantine, a hair brush, a toothbrush, toothpaste, his shaving kit and a bottle of cologne. After washing himself as best he could in the circumstances Albert lathered up and shaved in his characteristically meticulous manner. With a few vigorous slaps, he then splashed some cologne on both cheeks

Like his father before him Albert had not aged especially well. His grey hair was receding and his skin had become blotchy. Long gone were the striking good looks that had once made him quite a lady's man. He guessed that his penchant for cigars was probably doing him no favours – his wife, Annie, was frequently telling him that the smoke dried out his skin and made it look kipper-like and that it stained everything from his fingertips to his hair. Albert disagreed saying that if Churchill smoked the wretched things in such abundance they couldn't be all that bad. Annie disapproved of the cigars for other reasons too. She maintained that they were inappropriate and unbecoming. Although he treasured his cigar-smoking as one of his little pleasures in life, his excusable vice as it were, he had moderated his consumption in recent years.

Having completed his ablutions, Albert carefully unfolded his crisp white shirt and put it on. After adjusting his cuff-links and his navy blue tie he then went to the wardrobe and retrieved his three-piece suit, a plain, if not somber garment, which he donned slowly after checking, with some satisfaction, that the trousers had been properly pressed. Once he had finally put on his shiny black shoes he felt complete and ready to face the day ahead.

He checked his wristwatch. It was just after five o'clock. No rush. His nostrils told him that Miss Higginbottom was already up and preparing breakfast. She knew his requirements and was always very obliging. Although the smell of fried egg and toast should have been alluring, Albert often found the prospect of a hearty breakfast was too much for his stomach so early in the day. He nevertheless descended the stairs down to the small dining area where four tables were set for breakfast including a single setting for him. The room was poorly lit but neatly arranged. The walls were adorned with flock wallpaper and four rather amateurish water colours depicting gloomy forest scenes and seascapes.

"Good   morning   Mr.   Pointer,"   said   Miss Higginbottom using the false name that Albert always used on his excursions. "I've made your fried egg the way I know you like it, although I'm afraid that you only gave me enough coupons for one egg. I know you prefer two."

"No need to worry, Miss Higginbottom. No need to worry at all. A single fried egg will do nicely," replied Albert, carefully positioning a napkin around his collar so as to avoid any risk to his shirt.

"Down here for one of your sales trips I presume?" asked Miss Higginbottom as she handed Albert a weak cup of tea in a chipped china teacup.

"Yes indeed. Just a flying visit. I will be heading back to Manchester later on today."

"You must enjoy your work Mr. Pointer. It can't be much fun travelling the length of the country for business meetings and so on."

"I do my best Miss Higginbottom. I do my best. My wife misses me when I'm away but it's never for very long so it's not too bad. There are lots of people doing far more difficult and dangerous jobs than mine and no mistaking."

"More tea, Mr. Pointer?" she asked, directing the spout towards his cup in a way that suggested he had no alternative but to accept.

"Thank you Miss Higginbottom. You are most kind."

Having demolished the rather meager meal in a matter of seconds Albert played with the remains of the egg yoke with his fork. The simple truth was that he wasn't really hungry. He never was beforehand, although his father had always drilled into him that breakfast was the most important meal of the day and he took the advice to heart.

"Well, I'd best get ready. The car to pick me up will be here soon so I'll just nip upstairs and gather my things."

"Of course, Mr. Pointer. Don't let me detain you with idle gossip. I'm sure you've got important things to be getting on with."

Albert disappeared upstairs for a few minutes and then returned wearing his overcoat and hat. He could clearly discern the sound of the engine of the car waiting outside and fortunately the driver had the good sense to neither blow his horn nor ring the doorbell. There was no need to disturb anyone.

"Goodbye Miss Higginbottom," said Albert." See you again soon no doubt. Thank you as always."

"See you soon Mr. Pointer and good luck."

She was not the sharpest tool in the box but Albert often wondered if Miss Higginbottom knew a little bit more than she revealed. It was hard to tell but there was something about the tone of her parting comment that suggested this was so.

The driver of the black Austin A40 awaited Albert as he exited the hotel. The car's engine was idling but the driver stood on the pavement and opened the rear passenger door for Albert and then took his suitcase from him and placed it in the boot.

"Good morning," said the driver in a perfunctory manner, his short sentence accompanied by a nod. Albert responded with a forced smile. He entered the car without saying anything then sat down after removing his hat which he placed on the seat next to him.

Although the streets of West London were deserted, the driver had to proceed slowly because, notwithstanding the fact that the war had ended nearly a year ago, the roads were still littered with potholes from bomb damage. The shabby state of the street and the possibility of black ice called for caution. The driver had plenty of time and there was no need for undue haste. He headed westwards along the A402 and then turned north into Wood Lane. Apart from the odd milk-float and a refuse collection van there was precious little traffic around albeit that the first chinks of bluish-yellow daylight were just starting to appear on the horizon.

The driver suddenly broke the silence. "I'm afraid there might be a bit of a kerfuffle ahead Sir. We've had word that we may encounter a group of troublemakers outside I'm afraid. You know the sort Sir, do-gooders and so on."

"Indeed. We've had this kind of trouble before. Please ensure that the locks at the front are firmly secured. The ones at the back certainly have been. It won't be pleasant but I'm sure we'll cope."

As the vehicle headed west along Scrubbs Lane the bright searchlights from came into view, along with a silhouette of the archaic towers, the walls and the barbed wire. A jostling crowd became visible near the entrance. In the half-light of the car Albert reached for his wallet and checked the details on his train ticket that would take him back to Manchester. Assuming there were no hitches he would easily make it in good time the 11-40 from Euston. There was no reason why he should not.

He returned the ticket into his wallet and flexed his hands, once again making a clicking sound with his fingers.

THE TWITCH

For some bizarre reason the metronomic sound of the ventilator reminded Joanna of the dreadful piano lessons that had been foisted on her by her mother when she was eight years old. She had despised the creepy bloke who had taught her. What was his name? Colin. That was it. Creepy Colin. He had tried to impress upon her the importance of rhythm. He had a thing about rhythm that Joanna detested because she hated being forced to learn the piano and she hated Colin. She had matured since then and accepted that rhythm was alright insofar as it applied to Beethoven's Moonlight Sonata but the ceaseless pounding of the medical equipment that kept Stuart alive grated on her nerves even though it was, quite literally, the rhythm of life. She knew of course that if the pounding stopped then so too would the pounding of Stuart's heart and that at that point the absurd hope that a miracle might occur would be snuffed out. She didn't want that. Joanna kept on repeating the mantra to herself that where there's life, there's hope. And so it went on – Joanna hoping against hope that by means of divine intervention Stuart would somehow return from the twilight zone to which he had been so cruelly extradited.

Joanna had visited the hospital every day for the past two years. Seven hundred and twenty-eight days exactly. She had counted. And every single day she had sat by the bedside for at least an hour, talking to her husband and praying and talking to him some more. The army medical staff had done everything they could to help. They had flown him back in a transport plane to a proper English hospital and they had offered her every conceivable form of help and counselling but one simple truth remained: even though Joanna had spent more on flowers in two years than most people would spend on food, nothing had changed. Stuart's eyelids remained firmly closed and the motion of his lungs and diaphragm continued with the regularity and precision that only a man-made mechanism could produce.

And so it came to pass on a sunny Sunday in August that Joanna followed her usual routine. She arrived at the bedside shortly after eleven o'clock in the morning. The sun outside was terrifically bright and she adjusted the blind on the far side of the room to create some shade. She replaced the old flowers with a fresh bunch of red carnations and sat herself down on the chair next to the bed. She then produced two chocolate croissants from a bag which she placed on a napkin on the bedside table – one for her and one for Stuart. She fixed a small but powerful portable speaker to her iPad and set it to play a collection of her favourite songs. Stuart's face was a picture of serenity. She loved his features - his aquiline nose, his clear skin, his perfect lips. She cast around in her handbag for a small container of wipes and gently mopped his brow and cheeks. After doing this she started munching on her croissant and turned up the volume of the music.

"I've played all the music in your collection several times over," she said. "I'm afraid it has had no effect at all so I have decided to impose on you the most drastic of all musical remedies: Abba's greatest hits. Now I know you don't like Abba but I do and desperate times call for desperate measures. I'm quite sure that a heavy dose of *Waterloo* followed by *Dancing Queen* can only be a good thing. It certainly can't do you any harm, can it? Just accept that you're going to have to suffer this for the sake of the advancement of medical science and for your own wellbeing. I also know that you hate dancing but I well remember you rollicking on the dance floor at Pete's party when we first met. To this day I don't know if it was the tequila shots or an overwhelming desire on your part to impress me but you were certainly giving it your all when they started playing Abba songs. I wonder if you're not really a secret admirer? As I always do, I've brought you your favourite breakfast time treat – a warm chocolate croissant. If you wake up I promise that I will let you eat it in peace and switch off the music. I love you."

Joanna carried on talking over the music for just over an hour, stopping only when the album finished. She looked at her watch and reminded herself that she was due to meet her mother at one o'clock – Joanna had promised to accompany her on a shopping trip to buy a new washing machine and she couldn't keep her waiting. Joanna mopped Stuart's brow again and was just about to switch off the music when she noticed the forefinger on his left hand suddenly twitch. A shudder went through her. At first she thought that she had imagined it but then it twitched again. She stared at the finger and then at Stuart's face and then again at the finger. Stuart's face had not altered at all and now finger had stopped moving. Joanna drew breath and wondered what to do next. In two years she had not witnesses anything of this kind before; no hint that there was any real spark of life left in him. Nothing. This was truly extraordinary. After composing herself Joanna decided to walk out to the nurse's station and get some assistance.

"I must speak to Stuart's consultant Mr. Wells," she announced excitedly. "Stuart's finger moved. I saw it. This has never happened before. Can you call Mr. Wells?"

"I'm so sorry but Mr. Wells isn't in today. It's a Sunday. I will take a look and then we can call the registrar Mr. Franklin who is certainly on duty today."

The nurse examined Stuart briefly and ten minutes later the fresh-faced Mr. Franklin appeared and carried out a more probing examination, not just of the patient but of the medical equipment that was keeping him alive. He drew breath before speaking and pursed his lips as though poised to deliver some bad news.

"I don't want to raise your hopes Mrs. Abbott. As you well know it is extremely unlikely that your husband will emerge from his coma. The twitching in his finger was almost certainly an involuntary muscle contraction that signifies nothing. I hear what you say however and I will happily mention this to Mr. Wells when he comes in tomorrow."

"Mr. Franklin. I hear what you say and I'm glad that you hear what I say but please listen carefully. The man lying on this bed is my husband. He is not just a piece of meat. He is the man that I married and the man that I love. He is entitled to be treated with dignity, as am I. I am not someone who easily loses my temper but I am not prepared to wait until tomorrow. I would like you to do me the courtesy of calling Mr. Wells in order to see if he will come to the hospital today. Thank you."

Recognising the strength of the emotions that had been expressed to him, Mr. Franklin agreed to make the call and disappeared from the room, returning within five minutes to announce that Mr. Wells would come along within the hour. Joanna returned to the seat next to the bed and watched Stuart's body with great intensity for any further signs of life. Eventually Mr. Wells arrived, a lanky fair-haired man in his mid-fifties whose brusque manner had never appealed to Joanna but whose opinion she most certainly respected.

"What happened exactly?" he asked.

"His finger twitched several times but then stopped."

"Hmm. As Mr. Franklin has said, it could just have been an involuntary muscle contraction. As I've explained to you many times before Mrs.

Abbott, the chances of your husband waking up are very small indeed. If you look at him now you'll see that…hang on a second. Did you see his eyelid flicker? His right eyelid."

Joanna gasped and could feel tears welling up in her eyes. "I did. His eyelid did flicker and look at his finger. It's twitching again."

Mr. Wells checked a number of dials on the array of machines that surrounded the bed and made some notes with a pencil on a pad.

"Mrs. Abbott we'll carry out some more tests but please don't let me raise your hopes. These sorts of movement could signify one of two things. They could mean nothing or they could conceivably suggest that your husband's bodily organs, in particular his brain, are showing signs of recovery. The latter possibility is unlikely in the extreme. The harsh truth is that we don't keep any patient on a life-support machine indefinitely. At your insistence we've persisted with your husband well beyond the normal time scale. We've discussed before the need to make a decision about switching off the ventilator. We need to revisit that discussion. As you well know, he'll probably die if we do it. If however he starts to breathe independently then that would certainly represent a sign that he is, against all the odds, progressing. I can't guarantee anything I'm afraid and I appreciate that this is terribly difficult for you."

"What would you recommend?" asked Joanna, steeling herself for the reply.

"If it were my wife, I would switch off the ventilator but it is not my wife and I'm afraid it is not my decision."

"Then do it Mr. Wells. I have lived with Stuart's condition for exactly two years. If it is God's will that he should die then so be it. My personal view is that he was trying to communicate with us and that he will breathe unaided. I appreciate that a miracle is required but I have come to terms now with what we are all dealing with. Please proceed."

Mr. Wells summonsed two nurses and Mr. Franklin and after a short discussion in a huddle a few metres away he returned.

"I suggest we all sleep on it and reconvene at noon tomorrow. This will give us a chance to carry out some tests and will give you a chance to think carefully."

***

The next day, Joanna followed her usual routine and turned up at eleven o'clock with chocolate croissants, music and a willingness to talk. Just before noon Mr. Wells appeared with a junior assistant and two nurses.

"You don't need to say any more Mr. Wells. I stand by the decision I made yesterday."

"Thank you Mrs. Abbott," replied Mr. Wells who then turned to the more senior of the two nurses and nodded in the direction of the bed. The nurse then proceeded to flick three switches that obviously operated the ventilator. The group around the bed watched with grim expectation that the worst would happen. For several seconds Stuart remained motionless but then his chest started moving. Joanna stared in awe. Mr. Wells and the other medical staff did the same. A minute or so later, Stuart's shallow breathing had transformed into what looked like a normal pattern. He was alive. "This really is quite extraordinary," Mr. Wells added. At this moment Stuart's hands started to move and then both his eyelids followed suit. Joanna gasped but remained rooted to the spot. The senior nurse moved closer and as she did so Stuart's lips began to move. She placed her ear next to his mouth.

"He's trying to speak!" exclaimed Joanna.

"Well he's trying to whisper something – a sentence I think. It's hard to hear," said the nurse.

"Oh my God," added Joanna. "What's he saying?"

"It's very odd," replied the nurse, screwing up her face in bafflement. "It doesn't really make any sense. I'm not sure what he means. He just said 'I bloody well hate that Abba music. Please turn it off.'"

About the Author

Clive Zietman is a well-known litigation lawyer who lives and works in London. He has written several humorous books about how to complain under the pen name Jasper Griegson, including The Joys of Complaining and The Complete Complainer. He has been published widely in the British national press and has been a radio and television broadcaster for over twenty years. He will be donating all proceeds from the sale of this book to a spinal injuries charity.

17668403R00074

Made in the USA
Charleston, SC
22 February 2013